CHAPTER 1

COUNTY ANTRIM, IRELAND – OCTOBER, 1888

There was only one topic of conversation in the close-knit circles of the Ascendency in the north of Ireland for the better part of the autumn of eighteen eighty-eight, and that was Lord Deane Crenshaw, the Duke of Blackburn. More specifically, all high society could talk about was the fact that he had come to Ireland specifically to find himself a suitable duchess. An unprecedented number of balls had been put together, garden parties were as plentiful as clovers, and young ladies from every good family within a fifty-mile radius of Toome Hall, where the duke was staying with his aunt and uncle, Lord and Lady Toome, had been called home from whatever visits, finishing schools, and holidays they'd gone off on so that they could meet Blackburn and flirt shamelessly.

Because not only was Blackburn a duke, he was a duke with a scandalous reputation. And nothing was more worthy of gossip and speculation than a young, single duke with a scandalous reputation who was in search of a bride.

Deane was well aware of all of this as he was whisked from one cluster of beautifully dressed and coifed young ladies with stars in their eyes to another by his aunt at the musical evening she was hosting at Toome Hall.

"You have the pick of them, Your Grace," she whispered as she clung to his arm, glancing up at him. Lady Toome was startlingly short with light coloring, and Deane was over six feet, with black hair and blue eyes that betrayed his Irish connections, so the two of them standing side by side as they made their way across the room was an odd sight, as far as Deane was concerned. "Every one of the fine ladies here this evening is here for one reason and one reason only." She glanced up at him with coquettish eyes and a mischievous grin.

"To sample your special recipe for punch?" Deane asked, pretending to be utterly ignorant of his aunt's machinations, when, in fact, they weighed painfully on him.

"No, you silly." She laughed loudly, smacking his arm and drawing the attention of the dozen or more young ladies in the room. "But you have the right idea," she went on, lowering her voice to a whisper. "I should laugh

ALL ABOUT THAT DUKE

MERRY FARMER

ALL ABOUT THAT DUKE

Cover design by Erin Dameron-Hill (the miracle-worker)

ASIN: B08YX41BRN

Paperback ISBN: 9798519080835

Click here for a complete list of other works by Merry Farmer.

If you'd like to be the first to learn about when the next books in the series come out and more, please sign up for my newsletter here: http://eepurl.com/RQ-KX

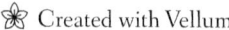 Created with Vellum

more at the things you say. That will make the ladies think you have a sense of humor."

"But I do have a sense of humor," Deane said in a low mutter, certain his aunt either didn't hear him or didn't have time for him to have a mind of his own.

As far as he was concerned, he had a very good sense of humor. He would have to after finding himself wrapped up in the comedy of errors that had led him to Ireland in the first place. A man had to be able to laugh at life when he found himself in a situation where he was seduced by one of the most worldly and sought-after widows in London to be her plaything for a summer. Lady Constantine had lived up to her name in that she had constantly wanted him in her bed or by her side at the opera, or entertaining the idea of running away to the continent together. Deane had been too flattered—and, unfortunately, too aroused—by the older woman's interest in him to say no.

A man also required a sense of humor to end up seduced again by his lover's rival. If he were honest with himself, he should have known what was about to happen when Lady Devereaux invited him to her townhouse, then insisted on interviewing him in the privacy of her boudoir. Even a dolt without Deane's Cambridge education should have been able to see that the second widow wasn't interested in discussing the politics of the day or getting his advice on the investments she claimed to have made. But, as usual, Deane had allowed his little head to do the thinking, and within a fortnight, the cat fight between Lady Constantine and Lady Devereaux over which of them should have the right to sink their claws into his flesh had spilled over into every drawing room in London and every scandal sheet in England, necessitating Deane's flight to his aunt and uncle in Ireland, at his eldest sister, Victoria's insistence.

He had to have quite the sense of humor not to dissolve into a pile of dust at the absolute disgrace he'd made of himself and the thoroughness with which he'd ruined his life.

"Ah, there," Lady Toome whispered, her hand tightening on his arm. "Lady Vanessa Rathkenny is free at last. She is the one I truly wish you to meet." She changed direction abruptly, tugging him over to the potted palms near the French doors leading out to the terrace, where a tall, willowy woman in a lavender gown that hinted the final stages of mourning, had just left off speaking with two other young women who had been thrown at Deane earlier.

Deane fought to smile instead of wince. "From the color of her gown and her decoration, I take it she's a widow?" he asked.

"She is." Lady Toome continued, slowing her steps, presumably so she could tell the whole tale before they reached the woman. "Such a tragic story, really. Poor Rathkenny adored her so, but he was struck down in his prime after being thrown from a horse while racing with his friends. Dear Lady Rathkenny has been left a widow at the tender age of thirty." She grinned broadly at

Deane, as though that were the best thing to ever have happened to either of them. "She still has plenty of child-bearing years left in her, and she has the social grace and understanding to make the perfect duchess."

"Does she?" Deane asked, squirming on the inside. Lady Rathkenny could have been the nicest woman alive, for all he knew, but his history with widows had him trembling in his boots.

"Ah, my dear Lady Rathkenny," Lady Toome beamed as soon as they'd reached the target of her machinations. "It is so good to see you out and about in society again."

"It is good to rejoin society, my lady," Lady Rathkenny said in a rich alto. She and Lady Toome exchanged polite nods before Lady Rathkenny lifted her hazel eyes to Deane. From the very first look, Deane could feel the matrimonial target shining on his forehead and Lady Rathkenny taking aim. "And might this be your esteemed nephew, about whom all conversation this autumn has been?"

Deane did his best to stand straight and smile as Lady Toome said, "Yes, this is His Grace, the Duke of Blackburn."

Deane wished his aunt would stop introducing him as though he were the Pope. He was only thirty-two and a duke by default, as the youngest and only male child of his dear, departed parents. Practically every other duke he knew was twice his age, and for once, he just wanted to be treated like any other man who still considered himself young and full of life.

"How do you do?" He bowed to Lady Rathkenny as formally as he could all the same, trying to smile when he was, in fact, in agony. He took Lady Rathkenny's hand and bowed over it.

"I am much better now," Lady Rathkenny said with that particular spark in her eyes.

Deane smiled, straightened, and glanced across the room for a way to escape. He also glanced around in search of another lady to talk to, a specific one at that— one he'd met briefly the week before at her sister's wedding. But he had yet to catch sight of Lady Chloe O'Shea at any of the numerous social events he'd been trotted out to in the week since the wedding.

Lady Toome cleared her throat, drawing Deane's attention back to the moment and Lady Rathkenny. "Well," she said. "If it's all the same to you, I'll just leave the two of you to become better acquainted. I see my husband fumbling about in conversation with Lady Coyle, and I feel I must come to his rescue."

"But of course," Lady Rathkenny said with a down-right wolfish smile. She hardly waited for Lady Toome to leave and didn't give Deane so much as a chance of starting the conversation before asking, "How are you enjoying Ireland, Your Grace?" She batted her eyes in a way Deane knew all too well as she asked her question.

"I...well...that is to say, I don't know how much of it I've actually been able to enjoy, since my aunt and uncle have kept me quite busy with social engagements," he answered.

"I see," Lady Rathkenny said, glancing up at him from under her lashes. "And have you found society in Ireland...engaging?"

Part of Deane wanted to sigh with exhaustion. He'd been through the same rigamarole Lady Rathkenny was attempting with him more times than he could count in the last few months, since the scandal broke.

"I have made the acquaintance of quite a few people," he said as politely as he could, hoping the woman would take the hint that he wasn't the cad his reputation had made him out to be. "I met a fascinating gentleman, Lord Caelian O'Shea, who is building a flying machine. I would love to learn more about that. And Lord Garvaugh took me on a tour of his estate the other day and showed me some innovations he has made to his farms' irrigation systems that I was quite impressed with." He prayed Lady Rathkenny would lose interest in him fast.

"That isn't what I meant at all," she said, dropping her voice to an even lower register and inching closer to him. She placed a gloved hand suggestively on his arm. "I meant, have you found yourself any particular company yet?"

It was all Deane could do not to roll his eyes. He decided to continue to pretend he didn't have a clue what the woman was suggesting. "I have been enjoying getting to know my cousins better, since we've only ever had reason to spend lengths of time together around holidays, when we are all in London."

Lady Rathkenny laughed as though he were a dimwitted child. "You have no need to pretend with me, Your Grace," she said, leaning closer still. "I am not a delicate maiden, like most of the ladies your aunt has introduced you to thus far. I was married for five years. I know the ways of the world, and your reputation precedes you." Her eyes glittered with lasciviousness.

"Does it?" Deane asked, roiling with discomfort.

"Oh, yes." Lady Rathkenny bit her lip. "It has been whispered to me that you are quite *talented*, and that you have been blessed with certain, shall we say, *assets* that do not leave a lady wanting."

Deane's face heated, and he wanted to sink into the floor. He was no more skilled than the next man who had more experience in bed than he should have. As for his assets, he was average, as far as he knew. Rumor and inuendo had a way of *expanding* things.

"Well," he answered, still playing oblivious, "I am quite good at cricket."

Lady Rathkenny sucked in a breath as though he'd said he was an expert at cunnilingus. "I look forward to putting your skills to the test, Your Grace." She went so far as to pluck at one of the buttons on his jacket.

That was the limit, as far as Deane was concerned. One little summer of mistakes, and now he was little more than a piece of meat for salacious widows to drool over. The whole thing was maddening.

"If you will excuse me, Lady Rathkenny," he said, glancing to the French doors behind them as one of the footmen tending to refreshments for the party escaped to the terrace, where extra bottles of wine and trays of snacks were being kept at the ready, "I need to have a word with that footman about a canape I sampled earlier that seems to have gone off. I wouldn't want anyone else to be made sick."

"No, not at all," Lady Rathkenny said, her eyes still sparkling, as though he'd made an assignation with her. "Perhaps we will see each other later?"

"Perhaps," Deane said.

He didn't waste any time. He leapt toward the door, slipping outside before Lady Rathkenny, or his aunt, or any of the other female guests who wanted a bite of him, could catch him and drag him back into the house. As soon as he was outside, faced with a startled footman, Gerry, he asked, "Which is the quickest way to get as far from the house as possible?"

Gerry laughed. "Head that way, straight through the boxwood garden. And if you're interested, since it's a nice, clear night, keep going up the hill and you might be able to see the meteor shower."

"Meteor shower?" Deane asked, striding swiftly in the direction Gerry had pointed. "That would be a damn sight better than anything going on in there." He gestured over his shoulder with his thumb, but kept walking into the dark, desperate to get as far away from mischief-minded ladies as possible.

. . .

IT WAS A BEAUTIFUL NIGHT, OR SO CHLOE O'SHEA told herself. It was warm for October, and the clouds had cleared midway through the afternoon, meaning she'd be able to watch the meteor shower after all. She'd gone so far as to strap her telescope to her bicycle and to make her way to the highest hill within a short distance of Dunegard Castle so that she could get the best view. She told herself that her choice of a hill that was technically part of Toome Hall, and within sight of the manor house there, was not because a very special evening of dancing and musical entertainment was happening there to celebrate Lady Toome's nephew, the Duke of Blackburn, whom she'd met at Colleen and Lord Boleran's wedding the week before.

She couldn't have cared less about such frivolous social events, especially when she hadn't been invited. She told herself she wouldn't have enjoyed the evening anyhow. The sun might have been in Libra, bringing balance and fairness to all things, but the moon, Mercury, and Venus were all in Scorpio, meaning everything would have been far too overwhelming and overstimulating for her. She was a Gemini, and Gemini and Scorpio did not mix well.

That didn't stop her from sighing and glancing down the hill toward the brightly-lit house. The house was easily half a mile away, but Chloe fancied she could hear the music of whatever orchestra Lady Toome had hired wafting through the night. And if there was one thing Chloe loved as much as she loved the stars, it was music. Even if she hadn't thought about Blackburn every day for the past week—since he'd caught her stuffing wedding cake into her mouth and come to her rescue by thumping her back when she'd choked on it—she would have liked to have heard the orchestra.

She sighed and dragged her attention back to her telescope. It was probably for the best that she hadn't been invited. People might have called her innocent, or even flighty, but she knew enough to know that Lady Toome did not like or approve of her. She was savvy enough to know that, even though her sisters, Marie and Colleen, had made brilliant matches within the last few months, that didn't mean the rest of the O'Shea family's reputation had been redeemed. They were still considered mad, bad, and scandalous to know, as that old poet was once called. She couldn't remember which one off the top of her head, since poetry had never been half as interesting to study as the stars.

She adjusted her telescope and gazed up into the heavens, searching out Saturn. There was something about looking at Saturn through her telescope that always thrilled Chloe. The instrument wasn't half as wonderful as the telescopes she'd seen the one time her brother, Fergus, had taken her to the Royal Observatory in Greenwich a few years ago, when they'd been in London. That single trip had ignited Chloe's interest in everything related to the stars. She'd only been a girl then, but she'd been allowed to look through Sheepshanks equatorial, an amazing refracting telescope, to see far out into the heavens. That one moment had made her feel infinitely small, and yet astoundingly powerful, at the same time. In fact, she fully intended to return to Greenwich someday to—

"Oh! I'm terribly sorry. I didn't mean to disturb you."

Chloe gasped and jerked back from her telescope at the deep, male voice that interrupted her thoughts. Her body flushed hot and cold at the idea of being caught trespassing. Those electric feelings only intensified when she made out the sight of Blackburn himself in the light of the single lantern she'd brought with her, which was secured to the handlebars of her bicycle, a few feet away.

"Oh, dear," she gasped, clapping a hand to her chest. "I...I didn't think anyone would notice if I set up here," she defended herself, certain Blackburn would take her to task. "This is the nicest hill within miles, and the heavens are so bright tonight. But if you want me to leave—"

"No!" Blackburn shouted, so loudly that Chloe jumped behind her bicycle, as if it could protect her from Blackburn's wrath. Not that it was wrath, exactly. "I mean, sorry, that was a bit too loud."

"It was, rather," Chloe panted.

"Again, I'm sorry." Blackburn took a step toward her, wincing. "It's just that I don't want you to run off on my account. In fact, I cannot believe my luck in finding you up here. I had to escape that abominable party, and there didn't seem to be any way to do it other than tearing off into the night. Gerry showed me how I could get away, and then I saw the light up here from your lantern...."

Chloe stared at him, not certain the man was making sense. He was a duke. *The* duke. The duke that every conversation had been all about for weeks now. And he wanted to get away from a party—that Chloe had not been invited to—in his honor?

"Anyhow," he went on, "I'm glad to finally meet you again, Lady Chloe."

"You remember my name?" Chloe asked, blinking.

Blackburn laughed. "Of course, I do. You made quite an impression on me at your sister's wedding last week. I was hoping we would get the chance to—"

He was halfway through his sentence, on his way to moving closer to Chloe, when he bumped into her bicycle in the dark, sending the whole thing tipping toward Chloe. The lantern crashed to the ground in a flare of burning oil between them.

CHAPTER 2

Finally, Deane felt as though he could breathe. It was more than the fresh air and the peaceful night. Lady Chloe O'Shea was every bit as charming and sweet as he remembered her to be. And he was unforgivable for startling her the way he had. He'd been so intrigued by the fact that the sister of an earl had set herself up with a telescope, alone, late at night that he hadn't thought to make his presence known gently. And then, as he usually did, he became overexcited when he thought he'd given her the impression he wanted her to go away. The truth couldn't have been more the opposite.

And then he'd gone and upset her bicycle, or more importantly, the lantern that had been sitting on top of it.

"Stand back!" he called, stepping around the contraption to grab Lady Chloe around the waist and whisk her away from the blast of burning oil. "You're all right," he said, keeping his arms around her and backpedaling.

In the process, he bumped into her telescope, knocking that over as well.

"Oh!" Lady Chloe gasped and pulled out of his arms, diving after her telescope. She had the fastest reflexes of anyone Deane had ever known and managed to catch the shiny, brass instrument before it could topple into the grass.

"Good catch," he called, as if he were at a cricket match and she'd stopped a ball from going over the boundary. "I would never have forgiven myself if something that precious had broken."

"It is precious," Lady Chloe said, sounding as though she were catching her breath in relief as she set the telescope upright again. "But it's also surprisingly sturdy. I've knocked it over several times, and it's been fine." She stopped with a slight squeak and straightened, glancing to the lantern fire—which had quickly burnt itself out on the damp grass—once she had the telescope back on its feet. "I hope my bicycle is undamaged," she said, crossing to the bicycle.

Deane cursed himself for doing nothing but standing there, staring at her while she spoke. Without the lantern, Lady Chloe was illuminated only by the bright moon and stars above, which gave her an otherworldly look. She was quite lovely, if he did say so himself. She was short, but she had the look of someone who spent a great deal of time outdoors, engaging in natural exercise—as opposed to the sallow, slender ladies he knew in London. Her face was round, and even in the dark, he could tell her cheeks were pink with health—and likely a bit of embarrass-ment, caused by him. She had beautiful, long, reddish-blonde hair as well, and whether it had come out of a style she'd had it in earlier, or whether she'd left it mostly loose on purpose, it fell in a captivating cascade down her back.

But he shouldn't have been staring at her and dreaming at all. He should be helping her, which was precisely what he had planned as he lunged toward her bicycle.

Only, instead of helping her reach for the contraption and pull it upright, he thumped into her, sending her reeling to one side.

"Blast it, I'm so sorry *again*," Deane said, cursing himself with his tone. "It's a good thing I didn't engage in any of the dancing at my aunt's ridiculous soiree this evening. I would likely have stepped on the toes of every woman she threw at me."

Much to Deane's surprise, Lady Chloe laughed. The sound was open and free, and it squeezed at his heart—and his balls—as it rang in the night air. "Forgive me," Lady Chloe said as they tugged the bicycle upright together, "but I suddenly had the image of Lady Toome lifting her female guests and bodily hurling them at you, like a caber-tossing competition I once witnessed on a trip to Scotland."

Deane laughed as well, charmed to the tips of his toes. "Have a care!" he called out jokingly, miming defending himself. "Here comes Lady Forsythe!"

"Duck!" Lady Chloe played along. "Lady Coyle has quite a bit of wind behind her."

"Oh dear." Deane stood straight, dropped his shoulders, and pretended to be staring up at a ceiling. "Lady Rathkenny seems to have caught her skirt in the chandelier. Is there a footman on hand to get her down, or shall we all find brooms and beat at her until she comes loose?"

Lady Chloe laughed hard, clutching her stomach. "What a sight that would be."

"We could sell tickets," Deane suggested.

Lady Chloe continued to laugh, but her cheeks suddenly seemed pinker, and her expression turned bashful. She cleared her throat and turned to survey her bicycle, propping it up again with a small, wooden stand he hadn't noticed before. "It looks as though the lantern fell far enough away not to burn any part of the bicycle."

"Which is a relief," Deane added. "I do apologize, deeply, for inconveniencing you." He walked around the front of the bicycle to survey the charred remains of the lantern. Oil was still burning in the grass, and if they'd been anywhere other than the top of slightly damp hill in Ireland, he might have been worried about a wildfire, but a few carefully placed stamps and flicking the ruined lantern out of the way with the toe of his dress shoes satisfied him that they weren't in danger of a conflagration. "We should keep an eye on that to make certain the fire doesn't flare up again."

"Yes, I suppose we should," Lady Chloe said, back to being guarded.

Deane regretted the tension that had flared between the two of them, and he didn't understand where it had come from. For those few, glorious moments, they had been enjoying each other's company in exactly the sort of way he liked to pass his time—easy, friendly, and humorous. He scrambled for something to get them back to that point, and pointed to her telescope. "What made you bring such a lovely instrument all the way up here to the hilltop?" he asked.

"I wanted to see the meteor shower," Lady Chloe admitted with what felt to Deane like a regrettable amount of sheepishness.

"Yes, Gerry—one of my aunt's footmen—mentioned there would be a meteor shower tonight," he said. "Have you seen anything yet?"

"A few meteors," she said, stepping back to her telescope and checking it over. "Although one doesn't need a telescope to see meteors. I thought I'd look at a few of my other, old friends while I was at it."

"You're friends with the stars?" Deane asked, grinning.

"Oh, yes," Chloe said. "We are on very good terms. You see Cassiopeia up there, of course. And over there is her friend, Lacerta, who I am also friends with, though she is better viewed through the telescope."

"Fascinating," Deane said, impressed by Lady Chloe's astronomical knowledge. "I know Ursa Major and Orion, but that's about it."

"Did you know that Orion contains a binary star?"

she asked, bending over her telescope to look through a small bit on top, then adjusting a few knobs.

"What's a binary star?"

Lady Chloe straightened abruptly and blinked at him. "You are a duke and you don't know what a binary star is?"

Deane laughed. "I'm afraid my education was mostly in the Classics and other useless information I might need when and if I sit in the House of Lords."

Lady Chloe shook her head scoldingly and bent over her telescope again. "All of that fine education wasted," she sighed, "when some of us are denied admittance to university entirely."

A sharp pang hit Deane's chest. "I take it you wanted to make a more formal study of astronomy, but were denied?"

Lady Chloe took a long time to answer as she sighted something with her telescope and fiddled with knobs. Deane could tell he'd struck a nerve, though. At last, when she straightened again, her expression held a great deal of regret. "Women do not attend university to study astronomy," she said, then stepped aside, gesturing for him to take her place.

"Nonsense," Deane said as he positioned himself correctly beside the telescope. "Women are being admitted to universities all the time now to study a great many things."

Lady Chloe cleared her throat as she stood to one side, her hands folded demurely in front of her. "Ladies are admitted to special colleges with carefully designed curricula. They are not permitted full matriculation in the way male students are, and certainly not at any sort of prestigious institute that teaches astronomy."

"I'm very sorry," Deane said, feeling irate on her behalf.

To his surprise, Lady Chloe grinned from ear to ear. "My, my, Your Grace. You do apologize quite a bit, for a duke."

Deane laughed, feeling his face heat, and hoping Lady Chloe couldn't see it in the darkness. "Dukes may apologize when they need to. But please don't call me 'Your Grace'. It's too formal, given the circumstances."

"What do your friends call you?" she asked.

For some strange reason, that simple question sent his heart soaring. It was astounding and ridiculous. Lady Chloe was a woman, not someone he would generally have considered a friend. He thought of telling her to call him Blackburn, like his school chums and other male friends did. But Lady Constantine and Lady Deveraux had also called him Blackburn, and the last thing Deane wanted was for Lady Chloe to remind him of that debacle.

"I know this is highly unusual," he said, squirming in his place a little as he did, "but for reasons I'd rather not discuss, even though it would be more proper, I'd rather you didn't call me Blackburn. So do you think, perhaps, you might call me...Deane?"

Lady Chloe's brow shot up and her eyes went wide.

"Not in public, I won't," she said. "I have enough black marks against me already."

"You do?" Deane asked, studying her with curiosity.

Lady Chloe's grin was as mischievous as it was wistful. "Haven't you been warned about that wicked O'Shea family since arriving in Ireland?" she asked. "Apparently, we cannot keep ourselves out of trouble, which means we are pariahs in the eyes of the Ascendency."

"You don't seem like a pariah to me," Deane said. "I found you charming at your sister's wedding, and I find you doubly so now."

Lady Chloe's mouth fell open, and even though they only had moonlight to see each other by, he could tell her face had gone red.

"I'm sorry, I know," Deane blundered on, wincing. "I don't think before I speak. Or before I act. It's gotten me into more trouble than you could possibly imagine."

"Trouble?" Lady Chloe's shock lessened, and she arched one eyebrow in teasing. "This wouldn't be the sort of trouble that I've heard rumors about, would it? The sort of trouble that brought a duke to far distant Ireland to find a bride who wouldn't mind a little trouble in exchange for the title of duchess?"

Deane sighed and let his shoulders drop. He dropped his head with them. "You've heard, then?" he asked, peeking up at her in embarrassment.

"I have heard that there was a bit of scandal involving two widows this past summer, yes," she admitted.

Deane had been embarrassed about the whole affair

—affairs—from the start, but never more so than with Lady Chloe standing across a hilltop from him, grinning as though the worst he had to confess to was stealing a pie from a farmwife.

"All right," he said, taking a step back from her telescope. "I'm going to tell you the truth about what happened, but only because I couldn't bear it if you heard the exaggerated version that seems to be making its way through all of Europe and believed that to be true."

"So you didn't have two, simultaneous affairs with two rival widows this past summer?" Lady Chloe asked as if it were nothing. "And it didn't cause a scene at a theater in Covent Garden that brought the opera you were attending to a stop while the two widows argued over you in public?"

"Er, well, um," Deane kicked his foot into the grass. "That did happen, yes."

Lady Chloe snorted with laughter, clapping her hands over her mouth.

"You're laughing at me," he said, genuinely stunned. "Laughing and not shocked or screaming, since you're alone with a man of questionable moral character."

Lady Chloe removed her hands from her face and arched one eyebrow as she asked, "Are you a man of questionable moral character?"

"No!" Deane answered, once again, too loud and too forceful. "No, I'm not," he tried in a softer voice. "But I do have my weaknesses." He cleared his throat, suddenly bristling with awkwardness. This was absolutely not the sort of conversation one had with a lady one barely knew on a hilltop at night during a meteor shower. It wasn't a conversation one had with a lady one had known for his entire life. "I let myself be led astray," he said carefully, hoping Lady Chloe was too innocent to know what he truly meant. "I failed to marshal my power to resist certain offers, and I suffered the consequences for it."

"I see." Lady Chloe crossed her arms and smirked at him. "You're lucky, Your Grace. Generally, when a woman fails to marshal those powers of resistance against those particular weaknesses, she ends up with child."

Deane dropped his head again, covering his face with his hands. So she did know what he was talking about. She wasn't a sweet, innocent flower who wouldn't learn about those things until her wedding night. He was genuinely mortified to have revealed all to her. And also immensely relieved, because Lady Chloe looked neither horrified by his revelations nor interested in throwing him to the grass, ripping off his clothes, and having her way with him, like Lady Rathkenny had.

"Can you ever forgive me?" he asked, peeking up at her once more, this time through his parted fingers as he continued to hide his face.

Lady Chloe laughed aloud at the picture Deane knew he made. She then surprised him by asking, "When were you born, Your Grace?"

"I told you to call me Deane," he said, then answered her with, "November seventh, eighteen fifty-six."

"Oh, I see," she said as though she did see. "That explains everything."

Deane lowered his hands. "Would you mind explaining everything to me?"

Lady Chloe's grin turned downright devilish. "You're a Scorpio. Passionate, powerful, and unafraid of the darker mysteries of the universe. Scorpio is ruled by the genitals, you see."

Deane nearly swallowed his tongue at her explanation, so fearlessly delivered. He didn't feel as though any of it applied to him, though. He was the most powerless man of his acquaintance, and he'd been so overwhelmed by the darker mysteries the dueling widows had opened for him over the past summer that he was now as far away from London and them as he could get. Although there was some truth to him being ruled by his cock, but wasn't every man?

"I had no idea I was so...easy to read?" He wasn't certain that was what he meant, but he was intrigued by what else Lady Chloe might think about him based on when he was born.

"It's not you...Deane," she said, looking scandalized at her use of his given name. "It's the stars. I don't just study their positions in the sky, I know quite a bit about what those positions mean and what they portend. I am not reading you, I am reading the stars."

Deane wanted to laugh, but he held back, thanks to the seriousness he could see in Lady Chloe's eyes. He wondered if she thought Astronomy and Astrology were the same thing. He also wondered if someone who had been denied the ability to study one would fall back on the other as a consolation prize. That opened his heart even further to Lady Chloe and made him want to know her as well as she seemed to think she could know him.

"What are you, then?" he asked, taking a step closer to her and ignoring the fact that he still hadn't looked through the telescope at whatever she'd pointed it toward. "Would I be able to know you if I knew the position of the stars at your birth?"

"Of course you would," she said, brightening for a moment before her face fell. "Only...." She let whatever she'd been about to say go with a sigh.

"Oh, dear," Deane said, stepping closer still to her, desperate to wipe the suddenly morose expression from her lovely face, perhaps with a kiss—even though kisses were what had landed him in such hot water to begin with. "Have I said something to upset you?"

"You haven't," Lady Chloe reassured him, smiling again, though sadly. "It's just that I'm a Gemini. And Gemini and Scorpio are not very compatible. In fact, they are decidedly incompatible."

"Are you certain?" he asked, inching so close to her that he could have drawn her into a passionate embrace with ease. "Because it seems to me as though the two of us are very compatible indeed."

She lifted her eyes to meet his with a combination of shock and arousal. And Deane was certain he wasn't imagining the arousal part. He knew when a woman was aroused. Lady Rathkenny had been earlier, but the sort of fire in Lady Chloe's eyes was far, far different. It was the sort of arousal that would lead him to do very bad things, if he let it.

"Do you know," she said, tilting her head to the side suddenly and blinking, "there must be something else in your star chart that makes the two of us compatible."

"My...star chart?" Deane asked. Lady Chloe was perfection. She was sweet, she was intelligent in her own way, she was completely artless, and she was beautiful. If Deane wasn't careful, she would charm him into a scandal even bigger than the dueling widows. The trouble was, he didn't think he'd mind a Lady Chloe-shaped scandal one bit.

"Yes," she said, gazing up at him intently. "It's a map of the heavens at the moment you were born. It's possible to determine all sorts of things about a person based on the positions of all the stars and planets in the heavens, as well as which planets and positions are in which house, at the time of one's birth."

"Is that so?" Deane caught himself brushing a lock of hair back from Lady Chloe's face as she stared up at him.

"If you gave me a bit more information—the time you were born and the location—I could calculate a natal star chart for you," she offered.

"I was born at my family's estate in Gloucestershire," he said. "And I happen to know, by pure coincidence, that I was born three minutes after midnight, because my father's birthday was the day before mine, and he always used to say Mama held me in until the next day just so I wouldn't have to share with him."

Lady Chloe giggled. "I'm not sure women are capable of simply holding a baby in out of spite."

"Not spite," Deane corrected her, tucking another strand of hair behind her other ear. "Teasing. Mama and Papa were forever teasing each other." He sighed sadly. "They were very much in love."

"That sounds like the sort of marriage I would like to have," Lady Chloe said. She was so unguarded as she spoke that Deane wondered if she realized how inappropriate the comment might have been, under other circumstances.

As it turned out, he was just as guilty of indiscretion. "I think that's the kind I would like to have as well," he murmured, his gaze focusing on her lips.

He wanted to kiss her. More than anything, he wanted to kiss her. No, in truth, more than anything, he wanted to lay her down in the grass and show her the true wonders of the universe. He had a feeling she would be game for it, no matter the circumstances or the newness of their acquaintance. But, he supposed, that was probably because he was a Scorpio.

That thought made him laugh in spite of himself, which made Lady Chloe laugh as well. Laugh and step away from him—which was probably best for them both.

"You still haven't seen what I aligned for you to look at," she said, bending over the telescope and adjusting it a bit. When she stepped back, she gestured for him to come take a look.

Deane did as he was told. He had a feeling he'd do whatever Lady Choe told him to do—and unlike the widows, doing whatever she told him to do wouldn't land him in the scandal sheets. When his sight adjusted to the tiny view through the telescope, he caught his breath.

"Is that two stars together?" he asked.

"It's a binary star," Lady Chloe answered. "Which, yes, is two stars that orbit each other, drawn and held together by their gravity. They will circle closer and closer to each other until, eventually, they merge into one."

Deane rocked back, smiling at her. He assumed that whenever the stars did collide, it would probably cause a moment of catastrophic explosion. But for some reason, that all seemed devilishly romantic to him.

"Blackburn!" a distant voice called out from closer to the house. It sounded like his uncle. "Blackburn, where are you?"

Deane cleared his throat and glanced guiltily to Lady Chloe. "I'd better get back to the party. It's being held for me, after all." He turned to go, then paused. "Do you want to come back with me?"

"Oh, no," Lady Chloe laughed. "I wasn't invited. Your aunt wouldn't approve."

Deane had a few choice words for his aunt in that moment.

"But if you'd like, I can bring your star chart over

tomorrow afternoon, once I've compiled it," Lady Chloe went on.

Deane burst into a wide smile. "I'd like that very much." He took a few more steps away from her. "I look forward to learning more about the stars," he said before turning and striding away.

And he looked forward to learning a great deal more about Lady Chloe O'Shea as well.

CHAPTER 3

*C*hloe had an exceedingly difficult time pulling her head out of the stars as she took down her telescope and fastened it to her bicycle—which was made that much harder without the benefit of lamplight. She'd forgotten about the brief fire entirely, thanks to the even warmer blaze of friendship and possibility that Blackburn —that is, Deane, though she didn't think there was any way she would ever have the nerve to call him that to his face in the daylight—had instilled in her. She left the broken pieces of the lamp on the top of the hill and pedaled home with a smile on her face and a thrill in her heart, repeating the details of Deane's time and place of birth to herself over and over so that she could calculate his star chart.

It was astounding to Chloe that an evening which had started out with such sadness and disappointment after being excluded from the soiree could end with such joy. After putting her bicycle and telescope away, she couldn't sleep—the same as if Deane had whisked her around the dance floor all night—so she got right to work on the star chart, pulling out all of the books of tables and maps of the heavens that she'd collected over the years.

By the next morning, as she joined her brother, Fergus, her sister, Shannon, and Fergus's wife, Henrietta, for breakfast, she felt as though she were dancing on air. She was even humming a spritely tune as she swept into the breakfast room, clutching the notebook that contained Deane's completed chart tucked against her heart.

"You seem to be in a delightful and cheery mood this morning, young Chloe," Fergus greeted her with a wry grin. He narrowed his one remaining eye, pointed his fork at her, and said, "What devilry are you engaged in?"

"Nothing?" Chloe sang. She set her notebook at her place, then drifted happily around the table to kiss her brother's cheek before continuing on to the sideboard to fix herself a plate. "It is simply a beautiful day is all. The sun is shining for a change—and it's in Libra, which always agrees with Geminis, like me—the grass is green, the weather hasn't taken a turn into coldness yet." She sighed as she plunked a few pieces of toast on her plate. "In short, everything is lovely."

She turned and floated back to her place, but before she could sit down, she noticed everyone at the table was staring at her.

Fergus cleared his throat and exchanged a look with

Henrietta. "Is that what it is?" he asked with a hint of teasing in his voice. "The sun in Libra?"

"Wasn't the sun in Libra when we met?" Henrietta grinned back at him adoringly.

"It couldn't have been," Fergus told her, managing to look like a lascivious pirate as he did. "We met in the spring, if I recall."

"I certainly do recall." Henrietta leaned over the edge of the table to kiss Fergus with a deep, flirtatious laugh.

Chloe grinned at her brother and sister-in-law, finding their love absolutely charming.

Shannon, on the other hand, cleared her throat and sent them a wary look before turning to Chloe. "How did you enjoy the meteor shower last night?" she asked.

"The meteor shower?" Chloe blinked, then remembered all at once the reason she'd gone up to the hill on the Toome Hall estate to begin with. "Oh! The meteor shower," she repeated. "Yes, it was quite lovely."

She attempted to hide her true feelings by pouring tea for herself from the pot in the center of the table, but she could feel her face heating far too much to escape notice entirely.

"I take it you found something of interest other than the meteor shower last night?" Shannon asked.

Before Chloe could answer, Fergus frowned at her and said, "So you are engaged in some sort of devilry after all."

"I am not engaged in devilry of any kind," Chloe said,

moving her notebook so she could shift her plate to the center of her place.

Although, if she were honest, Deane had looked devilishly handsome in the moonlight. He had the sort of dark-haired, blue-eyed appearance that she had always fancied—an appearance that made him seem full of life and mischief. And he'd been so honest with her about the scandal that had driven him to Ireland. Devils were not honest, so Deane didn't qualify for devilry.

A moment later, Chloe became aware that everyone at the table was still staring at her.

"I'm not in trouble," she insisted, trying to look indignant, but feeling guilty. She wasn't in trouble *exactly*, but even she had to admit that the entire interlude with Deane the night before was highly unusual.

Shannon, Fergus, and Henrietta exchanged looks. Henrietta—who always had been the most refined and well-mannered of them all—smiled kindly and said, "I see you have your astrology notebook with you this morning. Are we to expect a few predictions about the coming winter from the stars?"

"No," Chloe answered, buttering a piece of toast. "A friend of mine asked me to calculate his star chart."

Silence dropped around the table, followed by more exchanged glances.

"A friend asked you to calculate *his* star chart?" Shannon asked. "Is this a friend I know?"

Chloe pursed her lips and stared back at her sister, then took a bite of toast. She wasn't going to be able to keep her budding friendship with Deane a secret, much though she might have wanted to.

"If you must know, I encountered the Duke of Blackburn last night while stargazing," she said. "We fell into conversation, and as it happens, we have quite a bit in common. In the course of the conversation, I offered to calculate his natal star chart, and he welcomed the offer."

Again, silence.

"There truly wasn't anything inappropriate about the conversation," Chloe insisted. Unless one considered the fact that it happened in the dark, on a hilltop, and without the benefit of any sort of chaperone. All the same, when Fergus frowned at her, Chloe frowned right back and said, "I am not going to cause you the sort of scandal that Marie and Colleen did."

"No, you are not," Fergus said, as if it were an order. "Because unlike the muddles your erstwhile sisters found themselves in, it would be utterly impossible for me to untangle your knots by arranging for you to marry an English duke."

"And why is marriage suddenly part of the discussion?" Chloe asked, her cheeks burning. She had only just met Deane—well, she had made his acquaintance at Colleen and Lord Boleran's wedding—and she was far from contemplating marriage—although, with her sisters consistently being married off to the men they caused scandals with, that did seem to be something she should begin to consider talking about with her brother.

Fergus exchanged a look with Henrietta. The two of

them had a way of communicating without words that Chloe usually found endearing. In that moment, however, she found it frustrating.

"You are nearly twenty-three," Henrietta answered on behalf of both of them. "It is time for you to consider your future."

Chloe blinked in the middle of filling her fork with eggs. "Shannon is past thirty and she seems to be doing quite well for herself without a husband."

Fergus and Henrietta shifted their gazes to Shannon.

Shannon put down her silverware and raised her hands. "Please don't involve me in any matrimonial discussions." She pushed her chair back and stood. "I choose to be a businesswoman and not a wife."

"And what, precisely, is your line of business?" Fergus asked, his eyebrow above his eye-patch lifting.

"None of yours," Shannon said, returning Fergus's look with a sassy one before stepping away from the table.

In fact, Fergus knew that Shannon had continued the small brewery that she and the rest of the sisters had started when Fergus was still in England. None of them spoke of it, though, because prying Shannon away from the one thing that kept her from expiring with the boredom of the life a lady of title was supposed to live—as she described it—wouldn't have been worth the consequences.

"I need to be on my way as well," Chloe said a moment later, shoveling one last forkful of eggs into her mouth, gulping the last of her tea, and picking up her notebook in one hand and her last piece of toast in the other. "I need to deliver this star chart."

She stood, but Fergus stopped her with, "Chloe." Chloe paused and blinked at him. "I know you have a tender heart and a vivid imagination, but, darling, you cannot marry a duke. A man of that station will be looking for a woman who has been raised to manage that sort of a house and lifestyle."

"I wasn't planning on it," Chloe said, a little too high and breathless for her liking.

Fergus continued to stare pointedly at her. "I can work many miracles, Clo, but that's not one of them," he said.

"I...I know," Chloe said.

She clutched her notebook to her chest and marched out of the room. Just like that, she'd gone from soaring on the wings of happiness to crawling on the ground like the lowly worm everyone seemed to think she was. She headed out to the carriage house, where her bicycle was kept, alternating between sullenness and indignation at the way she was being treated. Not being invited to a soiree was one thing. It was Lady Toome's prerogative to invite or not invite whomever she wanted to her parties. Having Fergus tell her there was a limit to the kind of marriage she might have was a far bitterer pill to swallow. It felt too much like being told it was impossible for her to apply to university to study astronomy. She wasn't good enough for a first-rate education, but she wasn't good enough for a first-rate marriage either. Which begged the question of what she was good enough for.

The answer to that riddle seemed to fly at her from every direction. She wasn't good enough for anything.

Try though she did to shake the morose feeling those thoughts blanketed her with by forcing herself to smile up at the sun as she pedaled down the drive and along the road to Toome Hall, she couldn't quite banish the gloom from her heart. She reminded herself that she'd calculated her own natal star chart years ago, and it clearly showed that she was destined for great happiness and success in love and family. She clung to that hope as she pedaled up the drive of Toome Hall, rested her bicycle against the side of the manor house, and knocked on the door. The stars didn't lie, and they said she was more than worthy. That was why she loved them so.

"Can I help you?" the Toomes's butler greeted her with an imperious sniff.

"I'm here to see the Duke of Blackburn," Chloe told the man with her brightest smile.

Her brightest didn't seem to do a bit of good. "I will see if he is at home, miss."

"Er, that's 'Lady'," Chloe corrected him, surprised that the man hadn't even asked her name. "Lady Chloe O'Shea."

"Yes, I know," the butler said in a brittle tone. He hesitated, then stepped aside to allow her into the house.

Chloe swallowed the slight and said, "His Grace is expecting me."

"I'm sure, my lady," the butler said, as though he were anything but. "Please wait here."

He gestured toward a small bench just inside of the entryway. It was the sort of place where tradesmen or unimportant guests were asked to wait while it was determined whether the family were 'at home'. Chloe smiled in spite of the way her throat closed up in humiliation and shifted toward the bench. The butler didn't watch to see if she had a seat before striding off into the house as though he weren't in any hurry.

Chloe watched until he turned a corner, then sucked in a breath, hugging her notebook to her chest. She was the sister of an earl, for gosh sakes. And yes, she might have been the youngest sister from a family that had made quite a notorious reputation for themselves of late, but that didn't mean she deserved to be shunted to the side.

Indignation got the better of her, and with a quick look around to see whether she would be stopped, she tiptoed forward. It was still early for callers, but not so early that Deane wouldn't be up and about somewhere in the house. The butler wasn't quick to return, so either the family were in a far-off room or he'd been distracted by some other business. Either way, that enabled Chloe to creep down the hall, keeping her ears open for any sound that might help her find Deane.

It took less than a minute for her to hear Deane's voice. He was conversing with someone in one of the side parlors, likely his aunt.

"...yet another silly social occasion," he said, sounding unhappy with whatever was being discussed.

"These silly social occasions are precisely the way that you will find a suitable duchess," Lady Toome argued.

"There is nothing silly about any garden party hosted by me," a second woman's voice said.

Chloe would have known that voice anywhere. It was Lady Coyle, one of the most influential grand dames of the county. Lady Coyle fancied herself at the center of any event of importance involving the Ascendency, and she gave herself credit for half of the society marriages in all of Ireland. Knowing she was there had Chloe pressing herself against the wall beside the entrance to the parlor and holding her breath.

"I do appreciate your importance and your generosity, Lady Coyle," Deane said. "But I have been paraded around every social event and private meeting in County Antrim for the past six weeks. Is it so much to ask that I be given just a week to myself?"

"Yes, it is too much to ask," Lady Toome said. "You are not here for a holiday, young man. You are here because you utterly ruined your reputation, and your sister is relying on me to repair it."

"Time and perhaps a trip to the continent would have repaired it," Deane muttered. He didn't sound happy at all. Chloe couldn't blame him. She had the uneasy feeling that Lady Toome and Lady Coyle weren't thinking of Deane's wellbeing and future half as much as they were about how an association with a duke could benefit their social standing.

"Every young lady of good breeding has been invited to my garden party tomorrow," Lady Coyle went on. Chloe smirked to herself. She had not been invited yet again. "I don't see why you couldn't use this event to finally narrow down the field of your choices for duchess," Lady Coyle finished.

"Yes, it's about time we move on from finding your perfect bride to planning the perfect wedding," Lady Toome said with relish.

"Would it not be better to take some time to find the perfect woman for me to share my interests and my temperament?" Deane asked in a weary voice.

"Yes, that is precisely what I said," Lady Toome snapped.

"No, aunt, in essence, it is not," Dean said.

Lady Toome made an impatient sound. "Young men these days with their silly ideas of compatibility and *befriending* their wives." She snorted as though she didn't believe in either. "No, my dear, what you need is a woman of mettle and skill, one who is fit to be a duchess and to take society by storm."

"You need a woman who can rule you with a firm hand," Lady Coyle added, "since it has been clearly demonstrated that you cannot rule yourself."

"It was a brief period of very poor decisions," Deane said in an exhausted, suffering voice. "Am I to be punished for it for the rest of my life?"

"Yes," Lady Toome and Lady Coyle answered in unison.

"Now, I think we all know who the ideal candidate for duchess is," Lady Toome went on.

Chloe's brow went up. The wild thought that they might say her name struck her, as ridiculous as the thought was.

"Clearly, Lady Vanessa Rathkenny is the bride for you," Lady Toome continued.

Chloe made a sour face, as though the woman had suggested Deane suck a lemon.

"No, dear aunt, *that* woman is certainly not the bride for me," Deane said definitively.

Chloe was proud of him for knowing as much.

That pride turned to wary fear a few seconds later when the Toomes' butler rounded the corner and spotted her standing against the wall.

"Lady Chloe, there you are," he said, loud enough for everyone in the parlor to hear him.

"What is this?" Lady Toome asked.

Chloe could hear the woman crossing the parlor, so she jumped away from her pseudo hiding place and stepped into the parlor doorway with a bright smile. "Good morning, Lady Toome, Lady Coyle, Your Grace." She dropped into her prettiest curtsy, clutching her notebook to her chest. "It is a lovely morning, is it not?"

Her question, as feeble as it was, had the effect of putting Lady Toome on the back foot. "Er...um...I suppose."

"Ah, Lady Chloe, you've come at my invitation," Deane said, crossing the room to greet her with a smile. It was a clumsy greeting, but it conveyed the information to Lady Toome and Lady Coyle—and the butler, for that matter—that needed to be conveyed. "Do come in and join us. I've been expecting you." Deane reached for her hand and pulled her into the room with a hint of desperation in his eyes.

"I would be delighted," Chloe said, her cheeks burning with mischief. She certainly had the feeling that Deane was desperate to contradict whatever machinations his aunt and Lady Coyle had for him.

"You say that this...that Lady Chloe is here on your invitation?" Lady Toome asked as Deane gestured for Chloe to have a seat on a delicate chair beside an end table.

"Yes," Deane said, seating himself on the other side of the table. "Lady Chloe and I had a chance encounter yesterday in which she promised to calculate my star chart." To Chloe, he said, "I presume this is the chart?"

Chloe laid her notebook on the table. "Yes, it is."

"What, pray tell, is a star chart?" Lady Toome asked, moving to have a seat on the settee across from the chairs, where Lady Coyle was already seated.

"It is an astrological calculation of the heavens at the time of one's birth," Chloe explained. "One can learn quite a bit of information about the course of one's life by reading the stars."

"Oh, dear heavens," Lady Coyle said, rolling her eyes and pressing a hand to her forehead.

"And what do the heavens say about me?" Deane asked. He had a sort of eagerness in his eyes that thrilled Chloe.

"Well," she said, opening her notebook to the page where she'd drawn Deane's chart and removing the pencil she'd used to mark the place. "As we knew, your sun is in Scorpio."

"I beg your pardon," Lady Toome attempted to interrupt. She scooted to sit tightly on the edge of the settee. "We were in the middle of an important discussion, and we are not at home to callers."

"This will just take a moment, aunt," Deane said. "And what else can you determine from this chart?" he asked Chloe. He also took up the pencil and began to scribble on the corner of the page, his back angled toward Lady Toome and Lady Coyle.

"As you can see," Chloe said, her eyes wide, even though she tried to keep a straight face. "Your ascendant is in Leo. That means that you have a very forward and leonine disposition, and that you interact well with people, which would explain a few things." She grinned at him, knowing he would catch onto precisely what she meant by that. "And your moon is in Cancer, which means you feel things very deeply, you are quite emotionally intelligent, and you crave home comforts."

"I do crave those," Deane said. He moved his hand away from where he had been writing to reveal, "*I am*

43

*about to go mad with all of these marriage machinations
my aunt has thrust on me."*

It took everything Chloe had not to giggle. She took
the pencil from him and pointed at another aspect of the
chart. "Here you can see that Mercury is also in Scorpio,
like your sun. Which means you have a quick mind that
is not afraid of the darker side of things." On the paper,
she scribbled, *"What can I do to help?"*

"Is that so?" Deane took the pencil from her and
wrote as he spoke. "What about that curious symbol
there? What does that one mean?" He wrote, *"Come to
Lady Coyle's garden party tomorrow and save me from the
likes of Lady Rathkenny."*

"Oh!" Chloe gasped and took the pencil. She wrote,
"I'm not invited." Then she said, "That is the symbol for
Saturn. Saturn can be a difficult task master, and it often
shows where you may have to struggle with authority. As
you can see, it is also in Cancer for you, which means you
may have to struggle with your emotions and fight to have
them heard and understood, particularly by family."

"I do believe you're right, Lady Chloe," he said, then
wrote, *"Come anyhow, I'll vouch for you."*

Chloe beamed at him, but before she could reply in
any way, Lady Toome huffed and said, "Really, this is a
shameless imposition. Did you not hear me say we are not
at home to company today, Lady Chloe?"

Chloe took the pencil from Deane and closed it into
the notebook. She sent Deane a smile that was likely far
too open, then stood, clasping her notebook to her chest

once more. "I'm terribly sorry, Lady Toome. His Grace seemed so interested in knowing his star chart. It would have been gauche of me to deny his request."

"Poppycock," Lady Coyle sniffed.

"I have taken up far too much of your time already this morning," Chloe went on with her best apologetic look for Lady Toome. "I would not have imposed if His Grace had not insisted."

"And I did insist," Deane said, standing. "Lady Chloe, could I walk you out?" he asked.

"You will do no such thing." Lady Toome bristled in offense.

Deane offered Chloe his arm anyhow. Chloe took it hesitantly. "Thank you, Your Grace."

"Hennessey, see them out," Lady Toome called to her butler.

The presence of the butler made it impossible for Chloe and Deane to exchange any sort of meaningful parting, at least with words. Deane grinned at her as if they'd known each other for years and had spent weeks plotting the scene that had just unfolded. Chloe warmed inside and out at that show of confidence and friendship. She liked Deane. She liked him very much.

"Until tomorrow then, my lady," Deane said, letting go of her hand at last, once they reached the door. "And if you wouldn't mind, I would love a copy of my star chart."

"I'll make one up for you as soon as I can," Chloe answered with a broad grin.

"Thank you. But don't bring it to me at the garden

party tomorrow," he went on in a lower voice. "We'll save it for another day." He winked.

Hennessey cleared his throat as he held the door open for Chloe, but overall, Chloe didn't mind. She might have been dismissed from the house instead of invited in, but the short time she'd been there was all she needed. Deane wanted to see her again, and he'd indicated their friendship would continue. She couldn't wait for whatever might happen at the garden party.

CHAPTER 4

*L*ady Coyle's mansion stood on a slight elevation of green lawns and perfectly-tended gardens that looked out over a breathtaking vista ending in the Irish Sea. Deane was baffled that such a gorgeous setting could be the home to such a meddlesome old woman.

"Yes, yes, the Duke of Blackburn and I have become good friends over the past few weeks," Lady Coyle informed a circle of old women who had accompanied their husband-hunting daughters, nieces, and grand-daughters to the garden party. "I have exquisite taste in friends, you see," Lady Coyle went on, "and I believe I have earned a place as a trusted adviser to this young duke."

Lady Coyle's friends cooed and hummed over what they must have seen as the old woman's victory. Because if Lady Coyle was seen to have influence over Deane, she would quickly become the very best of friends with every mama who wanted a duchess in the family.

"I have enjoyed getting to know Lady Coyle," Deane replied with the sort of politeness that was expected of him. He didn't have to say any more, and part of him wished he could get away with saying a great deal less.

Sure enough, his simple statement caused one of the overdressed matrons to say, "Lady Coyle, have I told you how exquisite I find your gardens to be?"

"And that gown suits you so brilliantly," another rushed to compliment her.

"Thank you, Imogen," Lady Coyle said, then struck a pose to show off her dress. "I only wish that the weather had complied to make this the most comfortable selection for the party."

Deane hid his grin by taking a sip from his teacup. In fact, a slight cold snap had blown in overnight, making an outdoor garden party entirely unsuitable. But Lady Coyle had her plans, and heaven forbid Nature should get in the way of them. Deane glanced across the lawn, alternately sympathetic and amused by the tight clusters of ladies in gowns that would have been far more appropriate for the middle of summer. Those gowns showed them off to their best advantage, though—goose-flesh, hardened nipples, and all—so of course that was what the ladies all chose to wear.

"Your Grace, would you allow me to introduce you to my daughter, Lady Alison?" the woman whom Lady Coyle had addressed as Imogen asked.

Deane wasn't certain how to answer, particularly since Lady Coyle had a death grip on his arm. Imogen's earlier compliment must have done the trick, though, because Lady Coyle pried herself away from him and told her friend, "But of course you can," as though answering for Deane.

"I suppose I can," Deane said, trying to smile as Imogen hooked herself around the arm Lady Coyle had relinquished and tugged him off to one side.

From the moment he'd arrived, Deane had been dragged in one direction or another, introduced to ladies he'd probably met a dozen times already at events nearly identical to the one he was trapped in now, and fawned over in a way that made his skin crawl. And all for what? Not one of the ladies he'd been stuck in conversations with had the slightest idea who he was or what he truly wanted from life. All they saw was their chance to become a duchess.

"You know," Imogen said, slowing her steps as she walked Deane across the lawn to a giggling group of very young women, "I once had the interest of a duke in my younger years."

"Did you, Lady...." Deane bit his lip, scrambling to remember the woman's proper title.

"Lady Morrison," the woman said, not amused by his memory lapse at all. She plucked Deane's empty teacup from his hand and set it on the tray a passing footman carried, nearly upsetting the poor lad's load. "As I was saying," Lady Morrison resumed her almost flirtatious attitude, "I had the interest of a duke in my youth. He was a lovely fellow. Quite, *friendly*, if you know what I mean."

"I...er...."

"It was through that acquaintance that I discovered how very *friendly* I can be in return," Lady Morrison went on. She sent Deane a blatant look and batted her eyelashes. "It's a pity these young ladies are so necessary for continuing a family line when we all know that men such as yourself crave more experience."

Deane would have been surprised by Lady Morrison's clumsy attempts at insinuation if he hadn't heard the same from half of the widows—and several women, like Lady Morrison, who weren't widows at all—since arriving in Ireland. It was horrible. A few mistakes, and this was all he had to look forward to? And he was a man. He couldn't imagine the horrific way that young ladies who had made similar mistakes must be treated.

On second thought, he could. He'd seen the way Lady Chloe had been shunned from so many of the parties he'd been dragged to in the past few weeks. He'd seen the way his aunt and Lady Coyle had treated her the day before. And Lady Chloe wasn't even guilty of any sort of indiscretion. All it took was the ill-advised actions of her family, and she had been relegated to the status of a county joke.

"My dear, look who I have for you to say hello to," Lady Morrison announced to her daughter with a triumphant smile.

"Your Grace." Lady Alison and all of her friends dropped into short, shivering curtsies for Deane.

"Ladies, how do you do?" Deane addressed them all with a tight smile.

"We are a bit chilly," a raven-haired young woman answered him, immediately invoking the censure of her peers.

"What Lady Millicent means to say," Lady Rathkenny said—because, of course, the woman would be a part of the circle Deane had been led into, "is that we are all warmed and cheered by your arrival."

"Oh, yes," Lady Alison said, as though irritated she hadn't thought to say something similar first. "You are very warming," she added when her mother tapped her arm to prompt her to go on.

Deane roiled with discomfort. The whole party was so ridiculously awkward that he felt as though he might climb out of his skin. Who was foolish enough to plan a garden party in October?

"Perhaps Lady Coyle could be convinced to reconvene the party inside her home," Deane said, grasping at the possibility he could use the relocation of the party as an excuse to see if Lady Chloe had arrived yet. He had been looking for her from the moment he'd arrived, and with every minute that ticked passed, he worried she'd attempted to join the party and been turned away.

"I think that sounds like an excellent idea, Your Grace," Lady Rathkenny said, grabbing Deane's free arm.

"Why don't you and I search her out with the suggestion together?"

"Oh, well, I'm not sure that would be—" Before Deane could finish his protest, Lady Rathkenny had tugged him away from Lady Morrison—much to the woman's disgust, as proven by the ugly sound she made—and dragged him across the lawn. Her young friends looked put out but also impressed by their queen bee's daring.

"I could tell you were desperate to get away from that lot," Lady Rathkenny said in her low alto as they crossed the lawn.

"I hoped I wasn't that obvious," Deane murmured in reply.

"They are a dreadful bore," Lady Rathkenny said. "They can talk of nothing but the theater and dry old books."

"Oh?" Deane glanced back over his shoulder at the group. "Which books were they discussing? I have a fondness for—"

"There's no need to tell me how tiresome books are," Lady Rathkenny interrupted him. "You and I are the sort that find other things far more entertaining." She hugged his arm tighter. It could have been because of the cold, but Deane doubted it.

"I've always thought that if one doesn't enjoy reading, it is simply because one has yet to find the right book," Deane said.

"Tell me about your country estate," Lady Rathkenny

said, completely ignoring him. "It is in Gloucestershire, is it not?"

Deane sighed, knowing there was no way to escape the web he'd fallen into. "It is," he said. "We have the most charming lake on our property. I'm rather fond of rowing and fishing in the summer."

"What grand parties you must have," Lady Rathkenny ignored him once again. "I bet a man of your power and...*interests* hosts quite the bacchanals."

Deane gave up. His reputation had preceded him, and it had him in its iron grip. Women like Lady Rathkenny—and Lady Morrison—had their minds made up, and no amount of insistence that the most enjoyable pleasure he could think of was rowing his skiff out to the center of the lake on a summer's day so he could read something by Robert Lewis Stevenson would change it.

He had just resigned himself to the fact that Lady Chloe wasn't coming to the party, Lady Rathkenny wasn't interested in finding Lady Coyle and convincing her to let all the freezing ladies move inside, and his entire afternoon would be a miserable bust when Lady Chloe appeared on the porch that wrapped around the east side of Lady Coyle's mansion. The blessed woman wore a wool skirt with a matching, stylish, wool jacket. Her hair was caught up in a riot of light ginger with a pretty but stout hat pinned to it, and because the porch was several feet above where Deane walked with Lady Rathkenny, he had a glimpse of the thick-soled boots she wore as well.

"Oh, dear," Lady Rathkenny snorted at the sight of Lady Chloe, raising a hand to her mouth. "I didn't realize farm folk were invited to this party."

Deane dropped Lady Rathkenny's arm as though it had suddenly turned into an icicle. "Whatever do you mean?" he asked, raising his voice slightly so that Lady Chloe would be sure to hear him defend her. "At last, a lady has arrived at this party who is dressed appropriately for the elements."

Deane was certain Lady Chloe heard his statement, but her mouth barely twitched into a smile before dropping into a deeply anxious look. Deane stepped swiftly away from Lady Rathkenny, striding the short distance to the porch and mounting the stairs to meet Lady Chloe.

"I shouldn't have come," Lady Chloe whispered as soon as Deane was one step down from her. He stayed where he was, as it left their eyes level with each other. "I stick out in exactly the way that these sorts of ladies are always telling me I stick out."

"Because you have enough intelligence to recognize that it is, in fact, October and not July?" Deane asked with a wink, offering Lady Chloe his arm.

"Yes, and why is everyone dressed as though it is summer anyhow?" she whispered to him, stepping down to the lawn with him. "Aren't they afraid they'll catch their death of cold?"

Deane chuckled at her delightful practicality. "I do believe they're more interested in catching something else," he said, gazing fondly at her. "Something you seem to have caught the moment you arrived," he added.

Judging by the way Lady Chloe blushed, she caught his inuendo. The bashful smile she sent him in return was enough to have Deane's heart pounding...and his trousers fitting tighter.

"Your Grace, you know that there could never be anything between—"

"A Scorpio and a Gemini?" he finished her sad statement before she could become too attached to the idea that he was too far above her.

She broke into a gentle, self-effacing laugh. "Yes," she said. "We simply aren't compatible."

"But you said I have a Leo ascendant," he told her. "And a Cancerian moon. I looked those up, you know, and it turns out they are perfectly compatible with Gemini."

"You looked them up?" The look of hope she sent him was sweet beyond measure.

"Of course, I did," Deane said. "These things are important to you, so they are—"

"Good heavens. What is the meaning of this?" Lady Coyle marched forward from the group of matrons she'd been speaking with, fury in her eyes.

"Yes, I was about to ask the same thing," Lady Rathkenny said, crossing her arms and glaring at Lady Chloe.

"I do not recall inviting you, Lady Chloe," Lady Coyle snapped as she charged closer.

Deane felt Lady Chloe attempt to pull away from him, but he tightened his arm and closed his free hand over her hand in the crook of his elbow to keep her right where she was. "I invited her, Lady Coyle," he said. "I didn't think you'd mind a duke inviting a special guest." If he was going to have his title thrown at him every way he turned, then he would damn well use it to his advantage.

"Oh," Lady Coyle said, fluttering to a stop as she came near. The woman showed every sign of being in the throes of a mental crisis. "Well, I suppose, as a duke, if you chose to invite someone...."

"Lady Coyle, I was just observing that many of the ladies seem a bit cold," Lady Rathkenny interrupted. "Perhaps we should take the party inside and build up the fires quite a bit to warm everyone up." The way the woman stared at Lady Chloe, as if calculating how long it would take for Lady Chloe to overheat at an indoor party while wearing wool was diabolical.

"Yes, I think that would be a splendid idea," Lady Coyle said, a slow smile spreading across her face, as if she, too, understood the game. "Jankins, please gather everything up and bring it inside."

It was as though the lawn were a carpet and someone had lifted it up to shake the dust out. All of Lady Coyle's guests rushed toward the house as her servants and hired help gathered up refreshments and tables to take them up to the porch as well.

"This should be interesting," Deane muttered to Lady Chloe as they turned to head inside.

"It was your suggestion, after all," Lady Rathkenny said, sweeping up to Deane's other side to grab his arm. She glared across him to Lady Chloe as she did, then seemed to realize what she must look like and sweetened her expression. "How good of you to join us today, Lady Chloe," she said, baring her teeth. "And has your sister, Lady Shannon O'Shea, joined you today, or is she busy brewing beer at that quaint cottage the four of you used to live in?"

For the thousandth time since the party began, Deane wanted to sigh and roll his eyes. The games ladies played did his head in.

But Lady Chloe's answer pulled him back from the brink of hopelessness. "In fact, I do believe my sister is consumed with plans for her brewery today," she said. "She is quite close to finding investors to back her scheme. Did you know, Your Grace, that in the Middle Ages, brewing was an entirely female-owned industry?"

"Is that so?" Deane asked, brimming with affection for Lady Chloe and her determination in the face of impossible odds.

"It is," Lady Chloe said. "In fact, brewing allowed many women throughout the Medieval period not only to support their families, but to buoy the finances of an entire town."

"Oh, dear," Lady Rathkenny said as the three of them stepped inside the house, hiding her mouth with her hand again, as if Lady Chloe had said something gauche.

"It would appear Lady Chloe O'Shea is filled with every sort of knowledge."

"A trait that I find highly desirable in a woman," Deane said, grinning at Lady Chloe.

His words had every sort of effect he'd intended. Lady Rathkenny blanched and let go of his arm as they took up places near the freshly stoked fire in a large parlor, and Lady Chloe smiled knowingly, her already rosy cheeks taking on even more color.

Lady Rathkenny wasn't one to be held down, though.

"That is a brilliant idea, Your Grace," she said as though Deane had made some sort of suggestion. "We should play a game of wit and knowledge." She glanced around for support among her friends. Many of them looked to her, as though she were their leader, but few seemed to know what she was talking about.

"What sort of game of wit?" Lady Chloe asked warily, sending Deane a look as though she knew she was in for trouble.

"We should swap riddles," Lady Rathkenny said. She stepped away from Deane—who was forced to let go of Lady Chloe's arm as more people shuffled into the parlor —and moved to whisper in one of the other ladies' ears.

Deane knew in an instant something was being plotted in an attempt to set Lady Chloe in her place. He turned to her, hoping he could spare her any sort of embarrassment, but Lady Morrison had already grabbed Lady Chloe's arm to shuffle her as far away from Deane as she could get her. Fortunately, that ended up not being particularly far, since the number of ladies that had been invited to the garden party far exceeded the amount of space in the parlor.

"I will go first," Lady Rathkenny declared with a sweeping gesture, taking up the center of the room. She cleared her throat, then recited, "There is one that has a head without an eye, and there's one that has an eye without a head. You may find the answer if you try, and when all is said, half the answer hangs upon a thread!"

Deane grinned. He knew the answer to the famous Rosetti riddle. Surely Lady Chloe would too. What he wasn't so sure about was why the friend that Lady Rathkenny had whispered to earlier was now whispering in another lady's ear, and why they both continued the chain of whispering until it seemed as though some sort of nefarious message was being carried on the wind.

"Lady Chloe?" Lady Rathkenny asked. "Do you know the answer?"

"Yes," Lady Chloe said with a smile. "It's pins and needles. One has an eye and the other doesn't, and only needles, half of the answer, are threaded."

"Wrong," Lady Rathkenny all but shouted.

Deane went from smiling with pride for Lady Chloe to frowning at Lady Rathkenny in confusion. Lady Chloe was right. Everyone knew the answer to that particular riddle.

"The answer is tree branches," Lady Rathkenny said.

"Um, I do believe it isn't," Lady Chloe said in confusion.

"Lady Alison, do you have a riddle?" Lady Rathkenny turned to one of her friends.

"I do," Lady Alison said, stepping forward. "Which of the feathered tribe would be supposed to lift the heaviest weight?" she asked.

Deane's smile returned. He knew that one too. He'd seen it appear in various newspapers several times. He glanced to Lady Chloe with an encouraging smile.

It was obvious the others intended for Lady Chloe to answer, and without hesitation, she said, "A crane. Because it is both a bird and something used to lift heavy weights."

"Wrong!" Lady Rathkenny shouted a second time, even though Lady Chloe had the correct answer.

"The answer is Buffalo Bill," Lady Alison said. When several of the others glanced to her in question, she said, "I saw him and his tribe of feathered Indians when he was in London last year."

"But that's doesn't even—" Lady Chloe began to say.

"Lady Eveline, it's your turn," Lady Rathkenny turned to one of her other friends, sending Lady Chloe a wicked smirk as she did.

A young woman whom Deane assumed was Lady Eveline stepped forward and said, "Who killed the greatest number of chickens?"

Deane's mouth dropped open. Now they were simply toying with Lady Chloe, asking ridiculous questions that had no answer simply to embarrass her. Indeed, Lady Chloe clasped her hands to her stomach, dropped her head, and furrowed her brow in thought. Across the room, Deane spotted his aunt and Lady Coyle exchanging sly looks, as though they approved of the cruel behavior of the arrogant young women.

Deane had had enough. He was done with the joke that was being played on Lady Chloe, done with the airs and graces that the set of ladies his aunt seemed to think he should choose a bride from were putting on, and done with the way he was being treated as a prize for whichever woman slashed her claws through the others hard enough. The only woman worth a damn in the entire room was Lady Chloe, and he intended to save her.

But when he stepped forward, Lady Chloe raised her hand, warning him to stay right where he was, then lifted her eyes to stare right at Lady Rathkenny.

CHAPTER 5

*C*hloe took a deep breath to steady her nerves. This wasn't the first time she had been made an object of sport for the ladies of the Ascendency who thought they were better than her, and likely the entire O'Shea family. She'd been bullied by the women whom everyone praised as perfect models of female comportment for her entire life, and it burned like fire in her gut. She wasn't certain why her patience chose that moment to come to an end. Perhaps it was the way every young lady in the room seemed to be in accord with making her feel small. Or perhaps it was the way that Deane seemed outraged on her behalf, even going so far as to step forward, as if he would save her. But no, Chloe would save herself, and she would do it with finesse.

It helped that she knew the answer to the riddle Lady Eveline had asked.

"It's a reference to Shakespeare, of course," she said,

glancing first to Lady Eveline, then looking at Deane, as if explaining to him. She drew in a breath and straightened herself to her full height—which wasn't much—and tilted her chin up as she said, "The answer is King Claudius, Hamlet's uncle. Because he was guilty of 'murder most foul'."

A brief pause followed Chloe's correct answer. Lady Eveline dropped her mouth open and glanced to Lady Rathkenny, as if asking what she should do.

Deane laughed. The best part of that was the impression Chloe had that he was not laughing over the answer to the riddle as much as he was at her mettle in standing up to her bullies.

"Well, that's—" Lady Rathkenny started, as if she didn't know what to do when Lady Eveline failed to tell her she was wrong outright.

Before she could say more, Chloe cut her off with, "I have a riddle for you, Lady Rathkenny. One you may particularly identify with."

"Identify with?" Lady Rathkenny crossed her arms, glancing down her nose at Chloe.

"Yes." Chloe grinned at herself, knowing she was about to cross a line and not caring. "Who is Cerberus's mother?"

Lady Rathkenny blinked. A ripple of confusion passed through the room, and several of the ladies turned to whisper to each other, as though attempting to puzzle out the answer. Even Deane looked confused.

Chloe didn't give the assembly time to come up with

an answer of their own. "The answer should be obvious," she said, crossing her arms and staring straight at her rival. "You are, Lady Rathkenny."

"I am?" Lady Rathkenny blinked in surprise and touched a hand to her chest.

"Yes, of course," Chloe said. "Cerberus was a hell-hound, so of course his mother was a hellish bitch."

Dead silence followed Chloe's comment. Chloe's feet itched, and she figured she had about three seconds before she would be asked to leave. But she was surprised a moment later by a snorting laugh from one of the other young ladies near the back of the room. That burst of laughter was followed by another, then another, until a good half of the garden party guests were laughing *at* Lady Rathkenny instead of laughing *with* her.

"You must admit," Lady Coyle murmured, somewhat grudgingly, "that riddle wasn't entirely undeserved."

Chloe figured that was the closest she would be able to get to approval from the women of the garden party. She smiled as prettily as she could at Lady Rathkenny, then turned to march out of the crowded parlor and into the hall, telling herself she was looking for the tables of refreshment that Lady Coyle's footmen had brought up to the porch.

In fact, once she was safely away from scrutiny in the hall, she stopped to lean against the wall and blow out a heavy breath. What had she been thinking, coming to a party to which she hadn't been invited, with a bunch of women who looked down on her? How could she have walked into the trap Lady Rathkenny had laid out for her so blindly?

The answer poked his head around the corner of the parlor door, then walked out into the hall to join her.

"Lady Chloe, that was brilliant," Deane said, his eyes sparkling with mirth and approval.

Chloe pushed away from the wall and stepped forward to meet him in the middle of the hall. "I'm not certain it was the wisest or most mature course of action, but I refuse to be treated so shabbily by a woman who thinks far too much of herself, like Lady Rathkenny does."

"Well, I don't generally approve of jokes at the expense of others as a rule," Deane said, "because I have been the object of those jokes more often than not. But in this case, I am willing to make an exception, seeing as I agree with your assessment of Lady Rathkenny."

Chloe found herself grinning from ear to ear at that. Deane didn't think less of her for calling Lady Rathkenny a rude name. But she also wondered at his statement that he had been the object of cruel jokes before.

She opened her mouth to ask about that, but before she could get the words out, Lady Coyle stepped out of the parlor and into the hall. Lady Rathkenny was with her.

"There you are, Your Grace," Lady Coyle said with all the charm of an irritated schoolteacher. "Lady Beval was just inquiring about your plans for the remainder of your time in Ireland, and I said I would come fetch you."

"I am speaking with Lady Chloe at present," Deane said.

Lady Coyle marched right up to him and grabbed his arm, ignoring his statement. "I'm sure Lady Chloe wouldn't mind." She dragged Deane away from her. "Lady Beval is a dear friend of mine."

"You'd better go," Chloe told Deane in a quite voice that was almost a sigh. "I was just about to search out the refreshments myself."

"We will speak later," Deane said with a regretful smile, letting Lady Coyle lead him back into the parlor.

That, of course, left Chloe alone in the hall with Lady Rathkenny. Considering that was a situation Chloe had no intention of being in, she sent Lady Rathkenny a slight frown, then turned and walked away from her, searching for either refreshments or a way out.

"You cannot possibly think that the Duke of Blackburn will choose you as his duchess, can you?" Lady Rathkenny said in an acid voice, following her through a door at the end of the hall and out onto the porch. "Why, the entire concept is laughable."

Chloe told herself to ignore Lady Rathkenny's comment. The woman was likely jealous. Besides which, Chloe truly wasn't entertaining thoughts of marrying Deane, even though Deane was perfectly lovely and took her seriously, and they got along in so many ways. She was the daughter of an earl, after all, which made her at least a little marriageable. And dukes could marry whomever they wanted, high or low. So perhaps she did have to admit the idea of marrying him had occurred to her after all. It seemed very bold of her.

"You will give me your full attention when I am addressing you," Lady Rathkenny snapped as Chloe stepped up to one of the refreshment tables and reached for a teapot. "I will not be snubbed by a silly little nobody who gives herself airs and insults her betters in public."

Chloe huffed and turned to face Lady Rathkenny. "I'm sorry, but in what way am I lesser than you? I am the daughter of an earl, and if I recall, your father is a viscount."

Lady Rathkenny tilted her head up, her nostrils flaring and her eyes going wide before narrowing. "I am a countess, and my late husband was widely respected in County Antrim. Unlike you and your entire, scandalous family."

"Having a lofty title does not make a lady a good person," Chloe said, though she could already feel her courage draining away as Lady Rathkenny glared at her.

Sure enough, Lady Rathkenny took a few steps closer to her, towering above Chloe like a thundercloud.

"Let me make one thing clear to you, Lady Chloe," she said in a quiet, deceptively calm voice. "Your family may be titled. They may even have an income that allows them to keep pace with society. But that does not make any of you acceptable. Far from it." She shifted her weight in a way that made her seem even more menacing. "The name O'Shea is synonymous with foolishness and shame. Your ranks are filled with bastards and fallen women. Your lot are not worthy to sit at table with a duke, much less to marry one."

"I beg your pardon?" Chloe attempted to defend herself, voice shaking.

"Why do you think neither you nor your sister nor your cousins have been invited to so many of the events intended to introduce His Grace to suitable ladies?" Lady Rathkenny asked, then answered herself with, "It is because the very idea of an O'Shea marrying a duke is abhorrent. Not one of you comes close to suitable."

"That isn't fair," Chloe said, fighting not to believe Lady Rathkenny's words.

"Fair?" Lady Rathkenny reeled back with a derisive laugh. "Do you think it would be fair for an ignorant chit whose sister spent a night, unchaperoned, at the home of Lord Boleran to set her sights on a man like the Duke of Blackburn?"

"Lord Boleran and Colleen are married now," Chloe reminded her, not that she thought it would make any difference.

"Do you think it fair that a woman whose other sister connived her way into marrying the brother of her deceased fiancé so that she could snatch the title of countess should be allowed any title of her own?" Lady Rathkenny asked on.

"Marie and Christian were in love from the start, and it was only a misunderstanding that ended with her engaged to Christian's brother," Chloe said, knowing it was useless.

"And do you think it fair that a woman whose cousin throws away his money on some ridiculous flying contraption should have a place in the inner circles of English society?" Lady Rathkenny asked with a sniff.

"I think cousin Caelian has a very good chance of getting his dragon to fly," Chloe said.

"Do you think it fair that a man who so very obviously employs his illegitimate half-cousin as his valet should be considered honorable?" Lady Rathkenny continued.

"It isn't Avery's fault that Frank was born on the wrong side of the bed," Chloe defended her cousins. "I think it's extraordinarily honorable to keep Frank close to the family."

Lady Rathkenny snorted. "Listen to you? You're no better than a silly child. Everyone knows you're soft in the head anyhow, what with your stars and your parlor games and your belief in fairy tales."

"Everything we need to know about life and the expansion of the human spirit is in the stars," Chloe insisted, balling her hands into fists at her sides. "Someday, mankind will reach the stars."

Lady Rathkenny laughed sharply. "And you think you're worthy of being a duchess?" She grabbed Chloe's chin and forced her head up. "Go back to your nursery and your silly games, girl, and leave the real world to those of us who have earned it."

She let Chloe's chin go with a jerk that hurt Chloe's neck, then turned and walked back into the house. Chloe watched her with a tangle of emotions, despising the woman for her arrogance, but wilting because so much of what she said was true. The O'Shea family hadn't exactly made a sterling reputation for themselves. They were viewed as undesirable by far too many people in high society. It had never bothered her before, though. She'd always loved how creative and daring her family was.

At the same time, there was no way for her to deny the looks that had been thrown her way by Lady Coyle's guests. She and Shannon hadn't been invited to many parties of late. Even the Toomes' butler had sensed she was lesser somehow when she'd taken Deane his star chart. Chloe hated the doubt that seeped in through the cracks Lady Rathkenny had smashed into her, but there it was.

She couldn't stay at the garden party. Instead of fixing herself a cup of tea, as she'd intended, she marched away from the table and down the steps to the lawn. What was she thinking to believe she and Deane could be friends? His destiny was set, and so was hers, and those two paths would never cross, like stars occupying entirely different orbits.

She'd left her bicycle propped against a tree near the front door of Lady Coyle's house. It had been a bit of a risk riding to the party, dressed as she was, but she didn't care how high she had to hike her skirts up to avoid her bicycle wheels, the sooner she could get home the better.

"Lady Chloe, wait!"

Chloe stopped before she made it to the tree at the

sound of Deane calling after her. She whipped around to find him coming down the front stairs and striding across the gravel drive toward her.

"Your Grace," she said, continuing to move toward her bicycle, unable to manage even a small smile for him.

"I thought we agreed you would call me Deane," he said, lowering his voice as he caught up to her at the tree.

Chloe sighed and sent him a regretful look. "I'm not certain that's appropriate at this point."

Deane arched one eyebrow and crossed his arms. "What did Lady Rathkenny say to you?"

Chloe bit her lip, glancing back to the house. There was no telling who might be watching them or who might come charging out of the house to drag Deane back in at any moment. "Lady Rathkenny simply reminded me of our relative positions," she said.

"And what does a woman like Lady Rathkenny know about relative positions?" Deane said, as though Lady Rathkenny were the silly one.

Chloe managed a weak smile for him. "You are a duke," she told Deane, "and the most eligible bachelor in County Antrim at the moment. You could have your pick of ladies to be your duchess."

"Yes, I could," Deane agreed. Chloe began to deflate, until he said, "And in case you haven't noticed, I haven't picked a single one of them, even though I keep being thrown into their company. Honestly, it's been nothing but a trial for weeks. Do some of these mamas think I'm going to suddenly change my mind upon the fourth meeting with their darling daughters?" He made a dismissive noise.

Chloe laughed. "In fact, I do think they believe you will change your mind at some point."

"Well, I won't," Deane said. "Because for all their airs and graces, all of their breeding and training, I have yet to be even remotely interested in any of them. Not one of them has captivated me as fully as you have."

Chloe caught her breath and blinked up at Deane. "But as I've just been informed, I'm nothing but a silly little girl from a notorious family who isn't invited to parties because no one wants me there."

"I want you there," Deane said, sliding closer to her. He slipped a hand under her chin and tilted it up so she could look into his eyes. "And you're not a silly girl. You're a beautiful, interesting, free-spirited woman."

"But—" Chloe started to protest, but Deane stopped her with a kiss. The way he slanted his mouth over hers, brushing her lips lightly with his at first, then more insistently as he parted them, took her breath away. He traced his tongue along her bottom lip, then teased it against hers, coaxing her tongue into his mouth. It was beautiful and heady, and for a moment, it felt as though the world had stopped spinning.

As quickly as their kiss had started, Deane stopped it, pulling back.

"Oh," he said, cheeks going pink, eyes sheepish. "Forgive me, I got a bit carried away."

"I don't mind at all," Chloe sighed. She had her arms

around him, but didn't remember when or how that had happened.

"That's my problem, you see," he confessed, "and the thing that gets me into so much trouble. Sometimes I'm impulsive and do what I want before I think about it."

"You wanted to kiss me?" Chloe asked in a high, soft voice.

"I've wanted to kiss you from the moment I first saw you," Deane confessed.

"Then why didn't you?" she demanded.

She must have sounded too forceful, because Deane laughed. "Why indeed?" he asked, then leaned in to kiss her again.

It was sweet and beautiful, and made Chloe's heart sing. At the same time, she was all too aware of distant sounds of talking and movement from the back porch of Lady Coyle's house as her guests filtered outside once more. Chloe wanted to go on kissing Deane forever, but at the same time, she was loath to be caught.

"We can't do this here," she whispered, pulling away from Deane and reaching for her bicycle. "I have to go."

"When can I see you again?" Deane asked, stepping after her, but glancing over his shoulder at the porch at the same time. He must have been aware of the danger of being discovered.

"Um," Chloe thought as quickly as she could with her head turned with kisses. "Would you like to go for a bicycle ride tomorrow?" she asked. "If the weather is nice," she added. "And if you're free."

"I will make myself free," Deane said. "And I will use my ducal authority to ensure the weather is as beautiful as can be."

Chloe laughed. "All right, then. If you're able to pull it off, meet me at the end of the lane between Toome Hall and Dunegard Castle tomorrow around noon." She reached for her bicycle and wheeled it around. "Are you able to secure a bicycle for the day?"

"I'm sure I can," Deane said.

"Then I'll see you tomorrow." Chloe mounted her bicycle with a broad smile and sunshine in her heart. Her emotions had gone through so many swings in the past hour that she wasn't certain what she should actually feel about the rendezvous she'd arranged with Deane, but as she pedaled away from Lady Coyle's house, all she could feel was hope.

CHAPTER 6

*I*t took a great deal more finagling than he thought it should for Deane to convince his aunt to let him have a single day to himself so that he could meet Lady Chloe for their bicycle outing. He'd started by simply telling Lady Toome that he would be unavailable that day, but the way his aunt reacted, one would have thought he'd declared he had plans to meet Bismarck for tea. He'd thought about changing his story and telling her he was feeling ill, then sneaking out of the house to meet Lady Chloe, but that seemed underhanded —and his aunt was as likely as not to sit by his bedside, spooning gruel into his mouth if she thought he was ill.

In the end, Deane was able to secure a day for himself by promising to attend a special luncheon Lady Toome wanted to organize for the ladies she deemed most suitable for the role of duchess the following week. That luncheon would be long and painful, he was certain, but it would be worth it in exchange for spending an afternoon with Lady Chloe.

It was his aunt's suggestion of a luncheon that inspired Deane with the idea of bringing a picnic to his rendezvous with Lady Chloe. He discreetly had Toome Hall's cook pack a parcel with simple fare, which he managed to strap to the bicycle he borrowed from one of the stable hands. By the time he pedaled out to the end of the lane at noon, smiling up at the sunny, blue sky, Deane felt as though he'd orchestrated his own jailbreak.

"You see?" he asked as he rode toward Lady Chloe, who was waiting in the shade of a spreading tree, just off the road. He stopped his bicycle, standing with it between his legs when she turned to greet him with a joyful smile. "I told you that I would be able to wield my ducal influence to bring about a beautiful day."

Lady Chloe laughed. "I never doubted your power and influence for a moment, Your Grace."

The way she added his official form of address felt more like a private joke and a term of endearment than an honorific, and Deane loved it. Lady Chloe was the most beautiful thing he had ever seen, including the blue skies and green fields of Ireland around him. She was dressed in some sort of bright blue bicycling costume that involved bloomers as opposed to a full, long skirt. A woman like Lady Rathkenny would likely have found the style horrifically scandalous, but it suited Lady Chloe perfectly, and the color brought out the blue-green of her eyes. If Deane hadn't already been smitten, that would have clinched it.

"You don't approve of the bloomers," she said with a blush when she caught Deane taking in the full picture she made. "I knew I shouldn't have worn them, it's just so much easier to pedal fast in bloomers instead of a skirt."

"I absolutely approve," Deane said. "You're dressed appropriately for our activity, and you look comfortable as well."

"What is this?" Chloe's eyes took on a mischievous sparkle. "Is a duke actually approving of something practical and comfortable as opposed to opting for high fashion and expensive materials?"

Deane laughed. "I'm beginning to wonder if there isn't a vast conspiracy in Ireland to misunderstand dukes."

Chloe sent him a sympathetic look as she mounted her bicycle. They began to pedal slowly down the lane. "Do you know, I think there is a conspiracy, not to mention a great deal of misunderstanding, about people in Ireland in general."

"And how do you see this misunderstanding?" he asked, deeply curious to know what Lady Chloe thought, and about a great many things.

"Everyone seems to think that you must be very high-handed and imperious," she said, sending him a sideways glance as they pedaled up a small incline. Deane was impressed with how easily she took the hill. "The ladies at the garden party yesterday, for example," she went on.

"Judging by the way they all deported themselves, they must think every duke is a snob who cares only for wealth and status and who has no sense of enjoyment for simple things."

Her definition made Deane smile. "And you don't think I'm any of those things?"

"Of course not," Lady Chloe said with a smile. "I don't think any other duke is necessarily guilty of them either."

"I wouldn't be so sure," Deane laughed, relieved when they reached the top of the hill and could coast down the far side. "I've met a few dukes who were convinced of their own superiority in my day."

Chloe hummed. "They were probably Aries," she said. "Or Leo. Those sorts can be quite fond of themselves."

Deane laughed at her simple explanation for what he considered bad behavior. From her tone and facial expression, it looked as though Lady Chloe would be willing to forgive even the most boorish of men for their behavior, if the stars were right. Lady Chloe was the most forgiving woman he'd ever met, which was a quality he knew all too well was a rarity.

"I think the trouble is that far too many people see a ducal title as an indicator of the superiority of the one who holds it," Deane said. "And that is certainly not true."

"I agree," Chloe said as they sailed down the bottom of the hill and along a road that took them parallel to the sea. "I also think that too many of the ladies who wish to be a duchess want the title as some sort of proof that they are better than others. But only because they are inwardly so convinced that they are inferior at heart."

"What a fascinating insight, Lady Chloe," Deane said with a smile as they headed out toward a cliff overlooking the sea. "That those who are insecure seek outward validation to prove their superiority."

"I've seen it time and time again," Lady Chloe said with a shrug, or as much of a shrug as she could manage while riding a bicycle. "Unhappiness is a highly-contagious disease. Too many people believe the cure is money or a title, or criticizing others, or some other outward trapping of success."

"And what do you believe creates happiness?" Deane asked. "Let's stop for a minute over by that patch of grass," he added, pointing to the cliff.

They pedaled their bicycles to the promontory, then stopped. Deane unfastened the picnic he'd brought with them, surprising and delighting Lady Chloe as he did. The two of them spread the blanket and unpacked the meal before Lady Chloe had a chance to answer his question.

"What creates happiness?" Lady Chloe repeated the question once they were seated and gazing out over the sparkling sea, refreshments in hand. "Not titles and trinkets, that's for certain," she answered herself. "Not even good fortune and luck."

"No?" Deane asked, nibbling on the corner of the meat pie Toome Hall's cook had packed for him.

Lady Chloe chewed on her own pie with a thoughtful look before saying, "My brother, Fergus, is one of the happiest people I know, though he growls and frowns and carries on as though he isn't, if given half a chance. And yet, he is confined to a wheelchair, no longer able to walk, and he lost an eye due to a vicious attack several years ago."

"I'm sorry," Deane said, growing suddenly serious. "I didn't know he was attacked. I didn't think to ask what had caused his infirmities."

Lady Chloe looked downcast for a moment. "He was beaten nearly to death in England because he was Irish. But now," her expression brightened, "now he's one of the happiest men I know. And not because he's an earl or because he owns a vast estate in Ireland and one in England, thanks to his marriage to Henrietta. He is happy because he has a wife who loves him, children who adore him, sisters whom he vexes constantly, but who love him as well, and dear friends who write him copious letters and who keep threatening to visit." She grinned at Deane. "He is happy because he has love, every sort of love, in his life. Love is more precious than diamonds."

The way she said it, the way her smile reached deep into her eyes, illuminating her entire being, the way the sunlight played off of her ginger hair and made her seem like a being of light, all of those things had Deane's heart beating faster. More than that, he knew beyond a shadow of a doubt that if he had Chloe O'Shea in his life, he could be happy—dukedom or no dukedom. He could be a costermonger and still be the happiest man in the world, as long as she was his.

"My father believed as you do," he said suddenly, unaware of what was about to come out of his mouth until the words were spoken.

"Did he?" Lady Chloe asked with a soft smile, adding, "I assume he has passed away, seeing as you are the duke now."

Deane nodded, surprised both that thinking of his father made him sad and that he didn't mind feeling sad with Lady Chloe. "He and Mother both died two years ago during a boating accident."

"I'm so sorry," Lady Chloe said, reaching for his free hand and squeezing it. "I didn't realize you'd lost them at the same time."

"I did," Deane sighed. "And I was not ready to lose them. But they died together, doing something they loved to do. I should learn from that and seek to do the things I enjoy fearlessly instead of closeting myself away in society parties and other approved interactions that I despise."

"Like riding bicycles instead of attending garden parties?" Lady Chloe suggested with a grin.

"Precisely," Deane said, giving her hand—which was still in his—a squeeze. He grew a little more somber as he said, "And I do enjoy afternoon outings with a lovely young woman, discussing matters of importance, far more than stilted excuses for my aunt to lord me over her friends."

Lady Chloe laughed. "How very bold of you to say so."

"It's the truth," Deane admitted with a shrug. "And I feel as though I can speak the truth to you. I feel as though you won't hold it against me."

"Have people held the truth against you in the past?" she asked softly, finishing her lunch.

"Yes," Deane laughed bitterly. He turned somber again, then said, "So many people have and continue to hold everything against me for that embarrassing scandal with two older widows last summer, and it's wretched."

"You're such a Scorpio," she said with a sly grin.

Deane's heart flopped helplessly against his ribs. Lady Chloe's forgiveness was saintly and beautiful, which made him want to confess all the more. "I was suffering, you see."

"Suffering?" She raised her eyebrows questioningly.

Deane let out a breath, staring at their hands entwined. "I took the loss of my parents very hard indeed. I know I was twenty-nine at the time, but it was still a crushing blow. And yet, everyone around me, while sympathetic, treated me as though it were a stroke of luck for me. Imagine that, they'd say. Becoming a duke before you're thirty. You lucky devil."

"How horrible," Lady Chloe said in a genuinely sympathetic voice, inching closer to him across the blanket.

"I wasn't allowed to mourn," Deane went on, feeling rather as though he was stripping bare, but not in the good way. "My older sisters were. My nieces and nephews certainly were. But I was told to be the man of the family, to manage everything without breaking a sweat and to do so masterfully."

"Which I'm certain you did, no matter the pressures, because of the influence of your Cancer moon," Lady Chloe said softly.

Deane smiled at her in pure adoration, his heart blossoming in his chest. Her reasons for feeling confident in his abilities were super-natural as opposed to because he was a man and a duke and competence was expected of him.

His smile dropped a moment later as he rubbed his thumb over hers and said, "Some men lash out with violence or drink. I lashed out by accepting the first pair of comforting arms that feigned sympathy for my plight."

"One of the widows?" Lady Chloe asked.

Deane nodded. "And for God's sake, whatever you might think, please don't attempt to draw a connection between the loss of my mother and becoming the lover of an older woman," he said, wincing. The thought occurred to him more than a few times, and he was mortified by the implications. So much that he rushed on with, "I cannot help but wonder if becoming involved with Lady Constnatine's bitterest rival was my way of lashing out again when I discovered her affection for me wasn't genuine at all, and that I was just another trinket she'd collected."

"Oh, Deane," Lady Chloe sighed with such genuine feeling that it squeezed Deane's throat tightly. "You have been misused abominably."

"Don't try telling that to everyone else," he said with more than a little bitterness. He felt secure letting Lady Chloe see his true feelings, though. He was certain beyond doubt that she wouldn't judge him for them. "Everyone seems to think I'm some sort of a rake who delights in notching his bedpost with a string of conquests and who enjoys dragging out the process of finding a bride so that he can remain in the center of attention."

"But really, you just miss your parents and you want what they had," Lady Chloe finished his thought for him in a gentle voice.

It was too much. Unmanly tears stung the back of his eyes—tears of grief that he hadn't been allowed to express, and tears of absolute relief that finally, someone understood him. He refused to actually cry, but he came perilously close when Lady Chloe placed her free hand on the side of his face, then leaned in to plant a light kiss on his lips.

"You are allowed to be who you are, Deane," she whispered as she leaned back.

Deane shifted so that he could catch her around the waist and pull her close. "So are you, Chloe." She hadn't given him leave to address her by her given name, but he couldn't very well stop himself after everything they'd just said. All he could do was kiss her soundly, hoping she felt his burgeoning affection for her in every way.

A dog barking somewhere in the distance broke the two of them apart with the reminder that, even though their picnic was in a remote location, they were still out in the open. The last thing Deane wanted was for someone to find them and use all of the beautiful things growing between him and Chloe as more gossip.

He cleared his throat and said, "Perhaps there is a more private location we could move to."

Chloe grinned from ear to ear, impishness sparkling in her eyes. "I know just the place."

She leapt to her feet and helped him to gather up the remnants of their picnic and to fold the blanket. As soon as that was done, he fastened the basket to his bicycle and mounted it once more.

"You must promise me you won't be too shocked by what I'm about to show you and what I am about to suggest," Chloe said as they set off along the coastal road.

Deane laughed as he followed her. "After all of the confessions I've just made, you think anything you have to say could be more shocking?"

Chloe merely laughed in response and called over her shoulder, "I'll race you."

CHLOE'S HEART FELT BOTH HEAVY AND LIGHT AS SHE and Deane raced along the road to the cottage. He'd shared such intimate things with her, and those things were not the details of his tangled affairs. He'd shared his love for his family and his grief for his parents—two things that Chloe knew all too well herself. She felt honored and privileged that he would let her in to that part of himself, and she felt as though he deserved the same openness from her.

The cottage where she and her sisters had lived independently before Fergus had returned to Ireland was only a mile away from their picnic spot. They both pedaled furiously, laughing as the wind seemed to carry them along and flying across the colorful coast. Deane was clearly competitive, but seeing as he didn't know where they were going, he hung back enough to make it look like Chloe was winning. She adored him for it.

"That's the cottage," she called out as her old home came into view around a corner. "But be careful. By the looks of things, Shannon might be here, brewing."

"Brewing what?" Deane asked with a laugh.

"Why, beer, of course," Chloe answered, slowing considerably. When Deane slowed at her side, she said, "My sisters and I used to live here together. We dabbled in various hobbies and crafts, but Shannon in particular became extraordinarily adept at brewing beer. She still sells it to some of the pubs in town, and we help. She has it in her head now to expand the business into a commercial enterprise."

Deane's eyes went wide at the prospect. "Does she have any samples in the house?" he asked mischievously.

"She probably does," Chloe laughed, then stopped her bicycle entirely and dismounted to walk it off the path. "Let's keep out of sight so she, er, doesn't ask questions about why we might be here."

Deane caught on to her mischievous suggestion and grinned wickedly at her. "Good idea," he said, dismounting and leaving the path with her.

Shannon was, indeed, at the cottage, though by the look of things, she was just finishing up loading her latest batch of beer into one of Fergus's small carts. Chloe and Deane wheeled their bicycles silently around to the back of the house, leaving them propped against the wall, and spied on Shannon around the corner of the cottage.

"Your sister appears to be a mightily determined woman," Deane whispered, leaning close to Chloe.

"Oh, she is," Chloe assured him. "You've seen how people denigrate me for my fascination with the stars. Well, you can imagine what they think of Shannon for her determination to start a brewery."

"An entire brewery?" Deane asked, glancing from Chloe to Shannon as she finished loading her cart, then climbed into the driver's seat. "A noblewoman starting a brewery?"

"It's already started," Chloe said, raising her voice slightly as Shannon snapped the reins over her horse's back to pull the wagon away. "What she'd truly like to do is expand it into cities like Belfast."

She glanced anxiously up at Deane, who straightened and watched Shannon driving away with a look of amazement. Deane seemed almost perfect so far, but if he objected to Shannon's wildly unconventional plans for her life, Chloe feared she would be crushed.

"I don't understand," Deane said, pulling his glance away from Shannon and smiling at Chloe. Chloe nibbled her lip anxiously until Deane said, "I don't understand why everyone in this blasted county seems to think the O'Shea family is wicked and objectionable. If you ask me, you are the most fascinating, industrious, and entertaining group of people I've ever met."

Chloe broke into a smile that reached all the way into her soul. "Thank you so much for saying that," she said, throwing her arms around Deane's shoulders and lifting to her toes so she could kiss him. "It feels wonderful to have someone understand for a change."

"Yes, it does," Deane replied, wrapping his arms around her and kissing her in return.

His kiss was passionate and utterly inappropriate... for the standard dictates of society. Chloe didn't care a fig for those dictates, though. They'd never done her any good, and she suspected they'd never worked for Deane as well. What worked for them both was the way their tongues played with each other and their bodies heated as they embraced. Chloe loved everything about it, and about the internal closeness she felt for Deane, even though it could be argued they'd only met recently. Time didn't matter when fate took hold of the reins.

"Perhaps you could show me the inside of your lovely

cottage," Deane murmured, brushing the back of his fingers across her cheek, his eyes dancing with hunger.

Chloe giggled deep in her throat as she pulled back and took his hand, leading him to the cottage's back door. "Scorpios," she teased him, flirting right back.

The back door was locked, but the key was hidden in a special compartment Marie had once carved into the stonework just beside the door. Once they were inside, Chloe rushed Deane through the downstairs room like a whirlwind.

"As you can see, we had everything that we could possibly have desired here, including books, candles, and comfortable chairs," she said.

"I take it you did quite a bit of reading?" Deane asked.

"Quite a bit," Chloe confirmed, starting up the stairs once they reached the hall after a sweep through the parlor. "I'd show you the kitchen, but it's likely a mess with brewing equipment."

"I forgive you for omitting it from the tour," Deane said in a mock serious voice. "I believe I'll be more interested in the upstairs rooms anyhow."

Chloe had no illusions about what would happen when they reached her bedroom. In fact, she'd been wishing heartily for it from the moment she'd kissed Deane during their picnic. Just because she was a virgin didn't mean she was innocent, and now that she'd finally found a man she cared enough about to change the first part of that statement, she didn't want to waste any time.

"You're certain this is acceptable?" Deane said as soon as they were in her bedroom with the door closed, tugging her into his arms and molding her body to his. "I might be a Scorpio with a reputation for being a rake, but I'm not completely depraved."

"What if I'm the one who is completely depraved?" Chloe asked, stroking her hands up the front of his jacket, then unbuttoning it as she peeked coquettishly up at him. "I am one of those wicked O'Sheas, after all."

Deane laughed, then bent down to kiss her. There was more heat and urgency in that kiss than there had been in any of his other kisses, and it thrilled Chloe through and through. "I should probably make some sort of a moral statement and step away from you to protect your virtue," he said with a sigh, then kissed her again before working open the buttons of her jacket. "But to be honest, lovemaking is damn good fun, I enjoy it immensely, I'm good at it—" he arched one eyebrow salaciously, "—and I have a feeling you will enjoy it as well."

"I know I will," Chloe said, her whole body trembling in expectation. "And I trust you completely."

Deane paused his unbuttoning with that statement and gazed into her eyes with fondness that was almost heartbreaking. He seemed to hold his breath for a moment, and when he let it out, he surged into her, kissing her passionately. Chloe sighed with contentment, which quickly turned into another sort of sound entirely as he loosened her jacket and spread his hands across her breasts. It was no wonder ladies—and gentlemen—ruined themselves over such things. She and Deane had barely gotten started, and already she knew she would have let him do anything.

"This part is a bit anticlimactic," Deane said, a bit breathlessly, stepping back from her. "Everyone always makes it seem like undressing is some glorious, romantic endeavor, but it's actually awkward and time-consuming."

Chloe laughed, feeling fluttery all over. "Then perhaps we should just be practical about it, undress ourselves, and meet in bed." She nodded to her narrow bed tucked under the sunny window.

"Agreed," Deane said, loosening his tie.

Undressing might have been practical and utilitarian, but something about it felt wicked as Chloe raced through peeling out of her bicycling costume. Part of her thought she should have taken more care and folded her clothes neatly instead of just throwing them over the chair in the corner as they came off, but every time she caught a glimpse of Deane undressing over her shoulder or in the mirror over her vanity, her pulse sped up and her hands grew clumsy.

Deane shed his clothes faster than she did and slipped between her sheets before she was finished.

"That's hardly fair," she said once she'd removed her chemise and drawers and skittered across the room to her bed. "You're getting a far better look at me than I managed to get of you." And it was all she could do not to hug herself to hide her nakedness as Deane raked her with a look, obviously enjoying the sight.

"You're the most beautiful thing I've ever seen," he said in a rough voice, his face coloring with arousal. When he dragged his eyes up her form to meet hers, he added, "And I'm most certainly not." He threw back the bedcovers to reveal everything.

Chloe gasped at the sight of his naked and aroused body, clasping her hands to her mouth as her eyes went wide. He was gorgeous in every way, from the lean lines of his form to the dark hair on his chest, to his stiff and sizeable penis. Every part of her throbbed in excitement at the prospect of tangling up with him, but in spite of everything, that excitement manifested in a laugh.

"Chloe," Deane complained, flopping onto his back as if she'd dealt him a mortal blow. "That isn't the sort of reaction a man wants from the woman he's about to ravish into oblivion."

Chloe laughed even harder and climbed into the bed with him. The bed was small enough that the only position that felt natural for her was to straddle his hips and grin down at him. "How does this reaction suit you?" she asked, already knowing his answer when he sucked in a breath and grasped her sides.

"Brilliantly," he sighed, surging up so he could kiss her.

His kiss was bold and possessive. Every time he kissed her, it was as though he revealed a different part of himself, and she loved this part. She loved the way he was hungry for her, the way his hands seemed to work in concert with his mouth as they roved her curves and left her breathless and sighing for more. Her body seemed to know everything it wanted much more readily than her mind, as she returned his kisses on instinct alone. She wanted to demand everything from him, and she wanted to surrender to him completely, all at the same time.

Within moments, he muscled her to her back, arching his hips into hers in a way that parted her legs farther, and she loved it. She dug her fingertips into his back and pressed into him as he devoured her mouth with increasing ardor. It was as though she couldn't get enough of him, but she was eager to try. She welcomed the way he thrust his tongue into her mouth and panted with pleasure when he kissed and nibbled his way across her neck.

"Oh, yes, that's lovely," she groaned when he shifted low enough to close his mouth over one of her breasts. "Yes, keep doing that. Oh!" She yelped and her eyes went wide when he brushed his teeth lightly over her sensitive nipple. Her whole body seemed to react to the impish treat, and her sex throbbed.

When she dissolved into a wicked moan, Deane lifted above her, grinning down at her and laughing. "Are you certain you've never done this before?" he asked with a teasing look.

"On my life, I never have," she panted. "But I'm beginning to wonder why not. This is magnificent. I should have been making love to every man in Ireland."

Deane shook his head with a smile that radiated affection. "Minx," he said, then lowered himself to kiss her again.

As it turned out, all of the magnificent things they were doing were only a prelude to the true magic Deane had at his fingertips. He returned to kissing and suckling her breasts for a moment before trailing his lips and tongue down her belly toward everything that was aching and throbbing for him between her legs. She'd heard Marie and Colleen whisper about exactly the sort of thing she knew Deane had in mind, but she'd never dreamed it could actually be as wonderful as her sisters had insisted until Deane's mouth brushed against that part of her.

"Oh, yes," she gasped, barely able to keep still as he parted her folds in order to stroke his tongue directly against her clitoris. It felt so powerfully pleasurable that she knotted her fingers in his hair, uncertain whether she would use her grip to urge him on or make him stop if it became too much. "Yes."

She felt as though she might come out of her body entirely when he slipped his fingers inside of her while continuing to lick and suck her. Everything about it was pure bliss, and within moments, the coil of energy that had been steadily intensifying since she started removing her clothes burst into throbbing bliss. Chloe couldn't help but cry out at the sensation, which somehow made even better as Deane groaned with pleasure as well.

She'd brought herself to orgasm before, but never so powerfully, and never for so long.

"You are perfection," Deane panted as he shifted above her, before her body had fully finished throbbing for him.

He waisted no time pushing into her with a glorious moan of his own. The intrusion was strange and almost, but not quite, uncomfortable. She wasn't used to accepting a man that way, but it was Deane, and in her current state of transported bliss, as unfamiliar as the sensation was, she wanted all of it, all of him. So much so that as he moved in her with increasing speed and intensity, she moved with him, urging him on. Her body seemed to know instinctively how to meet his in a way that pleased them both.

"Dear God, Chloe," Deane panted as he thrust with abandon. "You are—"

Chloe didn't get an answer to what she was. Deane's passion seemed to crest like a wave rolling inexorably toward the shore, then crashing against the rocks with cataclysmic force. He jerked hard in her, then cried out as his whole body tensed. Then like the wave rolling back into the sea, he groaned and sighed and collapsed atop her in a way that she immediately decided she loved. She wrapped her arms and legs around him, wanting to keep him exactly where he was. The feeling of fullness, body and soul, that he gave her was better than anything she'd felt in her life, and nothing and no one would be able to convince her to give it up.

CHAPTER 7

*D*eane's mind was made up. Come hell or high water, he was going to marry Chloe O'Shea. She'd touched his heart with her understanding and forgiveness, and she'd thrilled his body with her openness and ardor in bed. She was everything he could possibly have asked for in a woman, more than he deserved, and nothing would stand in the way of him spending the rest of his life with her.

All of that was decided within the half hour that they lay tangled up together, drifting in and out of sleep, after making love. Even with the window closed, Deane could hear the sound of the ocean mingled with Chloe's soft breathing, and smell the salt of the sea along with that of her skin. For the first time in ages, he found himself in a state of complete relaxation and utter happiness.

"I hate the fact that we can't stay here forever," he sighed as he rolled her to her back and gazed down at her.

"Who says we cannot stay here forever?" Chloe asked sweetly in return, a mischievous spark in her eyes.

Deane laughed deep in his chest and bent down to kiss her. "My aunt, for one. She likely has a thousand, useless social events planned for me over the next few days. And your brother and sister would likely miss you if you never returned home."

"I'm certain Fergus could do without me," she said, though Deane wasn't entirely certain whether the wistfulness in her tone was compassion for her brother or a feeling that he didn't care whether she was home or not. He doubted it was the latter. He couldn't imagine anyone not wanting Chloe in their lives if they could have her.

He dipped down to kiss her again, feeling the tell-tale stir in his body that said if he didn't get up and dress, they'd be there for another few hours. "Forever will come soon enough," he told her, hoping she would understand the promise for what it was. He couldn't make any declarations to her right then and there. He'd promised his oldest sister, Victoria, that she would be the first to know when he'd made up his mind about a bride. But the sooner he sent that telegram, the sooner he could reintroduce himself to Lord Fergus O'Shea and ask for Chloe's hand.

"And now," he said, kissing her lips again, then her chin, then her shoulder, and daring to go so far as to momentarily suck one of her nipples, causing her to gasp, "we need to get up and go about our lives so that steps can be taken to bring those lives together sooner."

Chloe's eyes lit with sudden excitement, but she kept her lips pressed firmly shut. Which, of course, made it impossible for Deane to resist kissing them again until they softened and loosened and let him in. He let his tongue play with hers for a moment and pressed his body into hers, until she writhed and sighed under him, growing far too warm for either of their own good.

"No," he said, pulling up abruptly. "We have to get up. I've already put you in danger of consequences we can't erase, and it would be rakish of me to do it a second time."

"But we've already established that you're not a rake," Chloe said, sitting when Deane pulled back into a crouch. "And once more could hardly create more of a risk for that particular outcome than has already been created." She lifted to her elbows and arched one eyebrow at him in a way that would have made a practiced coquette green with envy. Chloe was simply a natural when it came to seduction.

"Is there something about Geminis that make them insatiable?" he asked with a laugh, risking one more kiss before forcing himself to get out of bed and collect his clothes.

"A bit," Chloe said with a regretful sigh, getting up as well. She turned to make the bed, but told him over her shoulder, "Perhaps it is our dual nature. I am both sweet and innocent, but also wicked and daring."

"And I like it." Deane dropped the shirt he'd just picked up back onto the trunk where he'd left the rest of his clothes and moved to take Chloe into his arms. He kissed her soundly, grasping a handful of her backside possessively as he did. As he suspected, Chloe didn't mind the gesture at all. In fact, she laughed as he kissed her. When that laughter turned into plaintive sighs, though, and when his cock responded enthusiastically, he had to stop. "Dress," he said, mostly as an order to himself, stepping away from her. "The rest will sort itself out."

Meaning that, the moment he fulfilled his promise to Victoria and sent that telegram, nothing would stop him from marrying Chloe as quickly as possible so that they could spend as much time as they liked in bed.

Parting from Chloe was the hardest thing Deane had done in a long time, particularly since, once they had left the cottage and had ridden their bicycles to the end of Toome Hall's long drive, it was impossible for him to kiss her goodbye. The best he could do was wave longingly to her as she pedaled on to her brother's estate next door. He watched her for as long as he could before riding on to the heart of Toome Hall. The sooner he returned his borrowed bicycle to the stable and the picnic basket to the cook, the sooner he could change clothes and wash up a little, then ride into Ballymena to send his telegram.

He nearly made it back out to the stable again before his aunt caught him in the hallway.

"Is it true?" Lady Toome asked.

A hundred different possibilities of accusations his

aunt could hurl at him raced through Deane before he asked, "Is what true, dear aunt?"

Lady Toome made an annoyed sound and marched the rest of the way down the hall to him. "Is it true that you spoke to Lady Chloe O'Shea several times at Lady Coyle's garden party yesterday? Alone?"

Part of Deane relaxed, feeling as though he wouldn't be caught for doing more than speaking to Chloe at a garden party. The other part of him was irritated that his aunt felt it was her business to decide whom he spoke to. "Yes," he answered, figuring there was no point in keeping his regard for Chloe a secret. "I'm rather fond of Lady Chloe."

His aunt made a scoffing sound. "As one is fond of a stray dog, I suppose."

Deane's eyes went wide in offense. He couldn't believe his aunt's audacity. Chloe was the daughter of an earl, not a stray dog.

But before he could come to Chloe's defense, his aunt went on with, "Of course, no one will think any less of you for not knowing that the O'Sheas are the wrong sort. You don't know any better, my dear. But I will tell you now, no good will come from you attaching yourself to such a nefarious family."

"Nefarious?" Deane asked.

His aunt clearly didn't sense the warning in his tone. "They are all silly and scandalous," she said. "The women behave more like bohemians, and the men involve themselves in ridiculousness such as flying machines.

No," she shook her head as though she'd proven her point, "when it comes to deciding on your future duchess, there is only one reasonable candidate."

"And who is that?" Deane asked in a grim voice, suspecting he already knew.

"Why, Vanessa Rathkenny, of course," his aunt answered with a smile. "She is beautiful, she is accomplished, and she already has exactly the sort of experience that a man like you craves."

Deane blinked at his aunt, praying he wouldn't get an answer he might regret when he asked, "And what, precisely, does that mean?"

For a moment, his aunt looked flustered for being called out. "Why, it means she already has experience running a grand estate, of course," she said, blushing and looking away. "Her late husband was well-respected in County Antrim and had quite a large property."

Deane doubted that was what his aunt was thinking. The very idea that his father's sister would even consider things that a woman like Chloe would blush over, that she would believe every gossip-monger's salacious rumor about him, made Deane want to race through the formalities of marrying Chloe so that he could leave Toome Hall sooner rather than later.

"If you will excuse me, aunt, I need to ride into Ballymena on an errand before the telegraph office closes," he said, marching past her.

"Before you go," Lady Toome caught him, forcing him to turn back. "Just so you know, I have arranged for us to dine with Lord and Lady Loughguile, Lady Rathkenny's parents, tomorrow night. Lady Rathkenny will be there, of course, so it would be the perfect time for the two of you to discuss future arrangements."

Deane frowned and pursed his lips. "Aunt Ermengarde, there will be no 'future arrangements' between me and Lady Rathkenny. Now, please excuse me."

Again, Deane tried to walk away, but his aunt called after him, "What do you mean by that, young man?" as though he were a lad of eighteen instead of past thirty.

"I think you are wise enough to answer that riddle on your own," Deane called back to her, continuing down the hall to avoid being stopped again.

He attempted to shake the irritation conversing with his aunt had left him with, forcing his mind to return back to the blissful afternoon he'd spent with Chloe. It was hard to crawl out from under the cloud of frustration his aunt had shoved him under, though, and he found that he didn't want to think too hard about Chloe while suffering under it for fear that he'd begin to associate the two feelings in his mind. Instead, he thought about Victoria and his nieces and nephews and what they would think of Chloe.

By the time he reached Ballymena, his spirits were almost recovered. One fleeting glimpse of Lady Shannon O'Shea and her now mostly empty wagon of beer in the mews behind one of Ballymena's main streets as he handed off his horse for safekeeping improved his spirits the rest of the way. From the look of things, Lady

Shannon had every bit of mettle that it took to run a brewery and haggle with pub owners, as she was doing now. He had half a mind to say something to her when their paths nearly converged as they both walked through the alley and out to the main street, but that would give away that he'd been to the cottage earlier and seen her.

Instead, he continued on to the post office, which hosted a small telegraph office where he'd sent messages back to his sisters in the weeks before. He noticed fleetingly that Lady O'Shea had business in the post office as well when he held the door open for her, but they parted ways as they walked toward different counters.

Unfortunately, Lady O'Shea wasn't the only person of Deane's acquaintance in the office.

"Your Grace, what a pleasure to see you," Lord Loughguile said, stepping away from a counter at the side of the room, where he had evidently been preparing a letter of some sort. "We are so devilishly pleased to entertain you for supper tomorrow evening."

"Thank you, my lord, for inviting me," Deane said, wishing there were a polite way to escape the conversation. Especially since Lady Shannon seemed to be listening, even though she was trying not to appear too obvious as she stood in the queue for the post office counter.

"I will admit, I haven't been paying close attention to my daughter's aspirations of late," Lord Loughguile went on, making Deane cringe even more, "but my wife assures me tomorrow's supper will be quite auspicious."

"Oh?" Deane asked, wondering how much of a fight

he should put up. The preening fool could grin and insinuate all he wanted, but he couldn't convince Deane to marry his daughter when Deane's mind and heart were already set on Chloe.

"Yes," Lord Loughguile said with a flicker of his eyebrows. "So if there is a question you wish to ask me now...." He spoke too loudly, as though he wanted everyone in the office to overhear.

Deane cleared his throat. "If you will excuse me, sir, I see it is my turn at the telegraph window."

He stepped away from Lord Loughguile as quickly as he could, shuddering over the thought that, if his aunt had her way, a man like Lord Loughguile would be family.

The woman behind the telegraph window was, in fact, ready for him, which relieved Deane beyond measure.

"I'd like to send a telegram to London," he said, taking out his wallet so he could be ready. "To a Lady Victoria Debenham, my sister."

"Very good, Your Grace," the young lady said with a bright smile, fetching the proper form.

Deane went on. "It should simply read, 'Dearest V, the choice has been made, wedding before Christmas'."

"Oh!" the telegraph woman gasped. "How lovely."

Deane frowned slightly, particularly when he noticed several of the post office patrons, including Lady Shannon, peeking in his direction. "Keep this in strictest confidence, of course," he told the telegraph woman.

"Yes, of course, Your Grace," the woman said, though she grinned as though she would rush home and tell her entire family as soon as she was able. "We have a strict confidentiality policy here at the telegraph office."

"Yes, of course," Deane drawled. And he could imagine just how far that extended. He could see full well that time was of the essence when it came to engaging himself to Chloe, and the clock was ticking against him.

CHLOE FELT AS THOUGH SHE WERE DANCING ON AIR as she bicycled home after her wicked afternoon with Deane. Truthfully, it didn't feel remotely wicked to her. Everything she and Deane had done felt like the most natural progression in the world. Deane was handsome and generous, talented and perfect in every way. She understood completely why two widows could work themselves into such a state fighting over him. At the same time, she knew that if she ever met either woman, she would rage against them for mistreating a man as wonderful as Deane. He couldn't help it if he had an amorous nature. They had misunderstood and mistreated the gift he'd given them by allowing himself to be seduced. Those two might have shared his body, but Chloe was deeply convinced that she was the only one with whom he had shared his heart.

Every doubt she'd had about whether she was the right sort to marry a duke blew out of her head with the sea breeze blowing through her hair as he pedaled home. She wasn't marrying a duke, she was marrying a gentle, sensitive, wonderful man. That he happened to have a title was incidental.

Her mood of elation continued into the evening, as she prepared for supper with her family and came down to join them in the parlor before Cook sent up word that the meal was ready. Which was why she was surprised when Shannon intercepted her before she could even reach the parlor with a stern and serious look.

"We need to talk," she said, grabbing Chloe's hand and leading her into the morning parlor.

"Is everything all right?" Chloe asked. "Has something happened with your business?"

"No," Shannon said, keeping her voice low as the two of them stopped in the far corner of the room. "I'm afraid something has happened with *your* business."

Chloe blinked in confusion. "But I am not the one running a business."

Shannon looked vexed for only a moment before taking both of Chloe's hands. With a regretful, sisterly look, she said, "Dearest, I know you are fond of Blackburn."

"I am exceedingly fond of him," Chloe replied, feeling herself blush deeply.

Shannon sighed. "I'm afraid he's engaged to Lady Rathkenny."

Chloe's joy and warm feelings thudded to an end. "I beg your pardon?" Dread pooled through her.

"I overheard Blackburn speaking to Lord Loughguile at the post office this afternoon," Shannon said. "Lord Loughguile seemed convinced an engagement will be announced tomorrow, when Blackburn dines at their house."

"I don't think that is true," Chloe said, less certain than she wanted to be.

Shannon continued to wince and squirm. "All of the evidence seems to point in that direction," she said. "Blackburn went on to send a telegraph to his sister, saying a choice had been made and there would be a Christmas wedding."

Chloe's heart lifted and slammed against her ribs with renewed joy. "He said that? A Christmas wedding?"

Shannon narrowed her eyes suspiciously. "Yes, but he also mentioned something about a lady with a name that begins with V."

Once again, Chloe's hopes crashed. "Are you certain you heard correctly?" she asked. Part of her believed she should come right out and tell her sister what had happened between her and Deane that afternoon. Another part of her raced through everything that had taken place, realizing that Deane had never actually proposed. He had never so much as used the word marriage or made a single promise.

He had spoken of the future, though, and Chloe was convinced he had meant that his intention was to marry her.

Now, however, doubt had entered her soul.

"I will admit that I was somewhat distracted by my own business," Shannon went on. "But I did hear Blackburn speaking to Lord Loughguile about supper tomorrow. And I am absolutely certain about the Christmas wedding. And you know everyone in Ballymena is convinced Vanessa Rathkenny has already staked her claim on the duke."

"I'm not so certain that claim is justified," Chloe said, withdrawing her hands from Shannon's. She frowned, chewing her lip, then murmured, "But I'm not certain any other claims on him are justified either."

She should have asked for more clarity and specificity before parting with Deane that afternoon. Her heart told her that Deane was not a rake and a rogue, and that he absolutely would not seduce her simply for the sake of spending an afternoon in bed with her.

Although he had been forced to come to Ireland to choose a bride because of a scandal involving two women in London.

A scandal that he had explained to her openly and in the most heart-wrenching terms. He had been nothing but honest with her, nothing but true.

But they had only known each other a short time. It could very well be that he had taken her in to get what he wanted.

Which seemed utterly at odds with what she was certain she knew about him.

The debate raging in Chloe's head was maddening. She hated even the idea that Deane might be playing her for a fool, just as she despised the fact that gossip and inuendo had instilled so much as a modicum of doubt in his love for her.

There was only one way to resolve the conundrum, as far as she could see. She would have to discover the truth for herself.

CHAPTER 8

The supper at Lord and Lady Loughguile's house was a disaster before it even started.

Deane spent the rest of the day after sending his telegram to Victoria happier than he'd been in ages and loads more certain about his future than he ever dreamed he'd be. He didn't even mind his aunt and uncle's incessant talk about which young ladies would be most disappointed once Deane announced Lady Rathkenny would be his choice of bride, he simply ignored them.

He had every intention of riding out to call on Chloe the next morning—even though he owed it to Victoria to give her a chance to respond to his telegram before speaking with Lord Fergus O'Shea—just so he could spend the day with her, but his aunt nabbed him before he made it to the front door.

"We've so much to do to prepare for supper tonight, and for the future," Lady Toome said with a sparkle in her eyes. "And it all begins with a trip into Ballymena to visit Lord Toome's most favored tailor."

"But I have no need of new clothing," Deane argued, attempting to walk past her.

"Nonsense," Lady Toome laughed, surprising him by hooking his arm and walking out of the house with him. "You will need every manner of new thing to make the best impression." The way she spoke sent chills down Deane's spine. Even more so when she went on with, "Christmas is only so far away, after all, and I'm certain you will need the finest tailoring money can buy for any *special events* this Christmas season."

Deane frowned and pursed his lips. So rumors of his telegram to Victoria had reached his aunt's ears, had they? He could see the persistence in Lady Toome's eyes —and the carriage already waiting for them in front of the house—and chose to make the best of a bad situation. He needed to go into Ballymena to check for a return telegram from Victoria, after all.

Unfortunately, what Deane hoped would be a quick errand ended up taking most of the day. Not only did his aunt march him through several tailor's shops and shops selling everything else from boots to boutonnieres, far too many of his aunt's friends just happened to be in town as well, which necessitated stopping for umpteen conversations and tea at more than one café.

Worst of all, there was no return telegram from Victoria. Deane wasn't certain he expected one so fast, considering his sister usually had her hands full with children and social calls and charity work. But he had been looking forward to her approval so that he could continue on with his plans. He had half a mind to forget his promise and proceed anyhow.

That course of action seemed like the best idea when he and Lady Toome returned home—with only an hour to dress and depart for supper at the Loughguile estate—and Hennessey discreetly informed him in a disapproving voice that that miscreant, Lady Chloe O'Shea, had attempted to call earlier, but not to worry, he chased her away.

Deane was inches away from calling the whole supper off, but, of course, his aunt's bullheaded wishes won out, and in short order, he was being escorted into the manor house at Loughguile Park by a young butler who looked like he knew a bit of juicy gossip and greeted by a family that cooed and crowed over him, as though he were their prize.

"I must say, I have been greatly impressed by you from the start," Lady Loughguile said with a simpering smile once they were seated at the supper table.

"Of course, you are, my dear," Lord Loughguile said in a gruff voice, already on his second glass of wine before the fish course was served. "He's a bloody duke." The man proceeded to laugh garishly, at least until silencing himself with another gulp of wine.

"You must forgive my father," Lady Rathkenny said from her seat directly across the table from Deane, sending him a saucy grin. "He does so enjoy life. But I'm certain you do as well." She raised her wine glass to him, then took a long drink while staring right at him. Somehow, the women managed to make the act of sipping wine look salacious.

Perhaps it was beneath him, but Deane took only the tiniest sip of his wine, then placed the glass far away from his plate and said, "I prefer beer myself. I hear there are some exceptional local brews to be had around Ballymena."

He wasn't certain Lady Rathkenny or her family—and it seemed as though the entire, extended clan had been invited to the supper, siblings, cousins, and grandparents included—caught the reference to Lady Shannon O'Shea. He didn't know how many people in the county were even aware of Lady Shannon's activities. An earl's daughter who brewed beer was likely as rare as a phoenix, after all.

"We will be certain to stock all of your favorite beers in the house going forward," Lord Loughguile said, saluting Deane with his wine glass. "Seeing as you'll be spending so much time here in the future."

Deane wanted to sigh inwardly. He supposed it would have been unlikely that Lord Loughguile wouldn't get the wrong idea about his telegram. That still didn't mean Deane could be manipulated into the fantasy that the entire family seemed to be living in.

"What are your plans for the future, Your Grace?" Lady Rathkenny asked, eyeing him as though he were more delicious than the main course that the footmen were in the process of serving. "One would assume you intend to spend a great deal of time in London." She sent an excited look to her mother.

"Yes, London has all the best shops," Lady Loughguile said. "And the theater. And all the best society. And I'm quite certain a duchess and her mother would be welcome in any house." She sent Lady Rathkenny a bright-eyed look.

For the sole purpose of being contrary, Deane said, "Actually, my plans are to spend most of my time in Gloucestershire going forward."

Lady Rathkenny and Lady Loughguile lost their giddy smiles and glanced to him, as if remembering he was the key to the future they were painting.

Deane went on. "London was the scene of a bit of embarrassment for me, and I have many things still to settle after my parents' passing. Besides which, I prefer the countryside."

"But you have a townhouse, do you not?" Lady Loughguile asked.

"I do," Deane answered hesitantly.

Lady Loughguile winked at her daughter and whispered, "We'll be fine."

Deane couldn't believe either woman's audacity. He hadn't given so much as a hint that he was halfway interested in Lady Rathkenny. In fact, the more she flirted and batted her eyelashes at him, the more she leaned forward and reached for things on the table so that he could have a clear view down her inappropriately low décolletage, the more he believed he might even despise the woman.

He attempted to bow out of the conversation by tucking into his supper as though it were the best meal he'd ever eaten—although it was quite good—but his attempts to keep his mouth full only barely kept him out of the conversation.

It was a mouthful of food that nearly caused a disaster when, as supper neared its end, Deane spotted Chloe's shadowy, angry face in the bottom corner of one of the dining room windows across from where he sat. Chloe's sudden appearance was so bizarrely incongruous that he nearly spit a mouthful of Charlotte Russe across the table. He ended up nearly choking instead.

"Good heavens, Your Grace. Are you quite well?" Lady Loughguile asked in alarm, looking as though she might stand and thump his back.

"I—" Deane coughed a bit more, reaching for the wine he'd discarded earlier and taking a gulp. That cleared his throat, but as he hadn't been drinking with supper, gulping even weak alcohol only made him cough harder.

He stood, pushing his chair back, and glanced toward the window again as discreetly as he could. Chloe's face was still there, looking furious. As soon as Deane met her eyes, Chloe raised a hand to point to the side, as if ordering him to find a way to come speak to her, then she disappeared.

Paradoxical relief spilled through Deane. Chloe

needn't have ordered him. He was as ready to flee the horrid supper as could be. He continued to cough, though it was a bit more of a show after the initial shock, and reached for the glass of water at his place.

"If you will excuse me," he croaked, pointing to the water, his throat, and then the door.

He stepped away from the table, taking the water with him and drinking a bit as he went.

"Are you certain you don't need help?" Lady Toome called after him, looking vexed that he would spoil her perfect plans.

Deane pretended to still be beyond the powers of speech as he shook his head and pointed to the water, then the hall as he passed through the door.

As soon as he was in the hall, he picked up his pace, striding on in the direction he thought Chloe must have gone, searching for a way out of the house. Much to his horror, he had just located a parlor with a set of French doors along the same side of the house as the dining room when Lady Rathkenny swept into the tight room behind him.

"You are a very clever man indeed," she said in a low purr, pursuing him across the room.

"I beg your pardon?" Deane asked, whipping around to face her and splashing water from his glass on his hand.

Lady Rathkenny slowed her prowling approach, swaying her way over to him with a sly grin. "You forget, Your Grace. I know your type well. My late husband was quite fond of these sorts of games himself." She reached him and plucked the glass of water from his hand, moving on to set it on an end table, then facing Deane again, her back to the French doors. "One or two of his friends were quite skilled at arranging clandestine rendezvous as well."

Deane's brow shot up—partially because of the wickedness Lady Rathkenny seemed to be confessing to, but also because Chloe popped her head out from the corner on the other side of one of the French doors. Her eyes flared with indignation as she pointed to Lady Rathkenny.

"I don't believe I know what you are talking about," Deane said, using the words to make a gesture to Chloe as though he had no idea what was going on.

"You've no need to play coy with me, Your Grace." Lady Rathkenny advanced on him again, her hips swaying in a way she probably thought was seductive. As she did, Chloe planted her fists on her hips in a movement that was a thousand times more endearing—and more frightening—than anything Lady Rathkenny could have managed. "You and I speak the same language. We are both sophisticated people of experience."

"I'm afraid rumors of my experience have been greatly exaggerated," Deane said, sidestepping to get away from Lady Rathkenny when she was close enough to touch him. "I believe there has been a grievous misunderstanding here." He adjusted his position so that Lady Rathkenny would have no reason to turn toward the French doors and see Chloe.

"There is no misunderstanding," Lady Rathkenny said. "I know what I want, and I know what you want as well." She brushed a hand over her low neckline. "And believe me, I am willing to give you whatever you want. Right now, if you'd like." She glanced sideways to the settee, then surged toward him.

"God, no," Deane blurted before he could check himself, leaping so that the settee stood between the two of them. It felt like a cowardly move, so he cleared his throat and said, "That is, I am afraid you are operating under the mistaken assumption that I am the sort of man who conducts illicit affairs in public spaces."

"We could retire to one of my family's bedchambers, if you'd prefer," Lady Rathkenny said with a predatory glow in her eyes. "Mama certainly wouldn't mind. In fact, I think she's rather hoping we take our time rejoining the others."

"I—" Deane's mouth flapped open, but between his shock and outrage, he couldn't think of how to reply. Finally, he closed his mouth with a sigh and pressed his fingertips to his temples. "No, what I meant was, you've mistaken me for the sort of man I'm not."

"You are a duke." Lady Rathkenny shrugged one shoulder. The gesture seemed to remind her that her shoulder was there, and she lifted a hand to push the edge of her gown down, exposing said shoulder. She lifted her eyes to meet his with a heated look. "And you are a man whose prowess has so very many ladies in a tizzy." She pushed her dress off of her other shoulder, which caused the entire bodice to sag.

Deane wasn't made of stone, and perhaps under other circumstances, a lady attempting to disrobe in front of him would have led him to throw caution to the wind. Under present circumstances, however, knowing the matrimonial trap that Lady Rathkenny had set with herself as bait, a glimpse of pale shoulders revolted him.

"Lady Rathkenny, please," he said, standing tall, his back going stiff. "Enough of this. I find nothing at all about you throwing yourself at me so desperately to be the least bit appealing."

Lady Rathkenny blinked in shock. "I beg your pardon?" Her expression turned offended, but her cheeks flared pink, as if she knew she were caught.

"I am not the rake everyone seems to think I am," Deane defended himself. "And I don't know where you and your family—and my aunt, for that matter—latched onto the idea that some sort of marriage between us is imminent, but I can assure you, no such thing is about to happen."

"But I was given to understand...." Lady Rathkenny seemed to catch herself being too emotional and snapped her mouth shut. She pulled herself together and went on with, "My father assures me that a telegram was sent."

"Your father misunderstood the object of the telegram," Deane said. "At no point have I expressed any intention of marrying you."

"Who is she, then?" Lady Rathkenny demanded,

eyes and nostrils flaring. She didn't wait for Deane to answer. Instead, she stepped forward to say, "Whoever she is, you are making a mistake. There isn't a lady in this county who is more suitable to be a duchess than I am."

"That may be the case—" Deane began.

"You think you can do better than me?" she cut him off. "Who else among the simpering flowers and empty-headed maidens whose acquaintance you have made has experience with managing a vast and complicated estate? Who else is well-versed in the arts of pleasing a ravenous husband? Who else can keep up with the social demands placed upon a duchess and her family?"

"Those considerations have nothing to do with anything," Deane sighed. He could see that whatever argument he mounted, it was going to fall on deaf ears.

"Those should be the only considerations you have," Lady Rathkenny insisted. She darted around the settee toward him, clasping onto his lapels. Deane glanced desperately toward the French doors, but Chloe was no longer there. "Is it sexual favors you're after?" Lady Rathkenny asked on. "I am willing to do things other women wouldn't do. Here, let me show you."

She attempted to drop to her knees before him, reaching for the fastenings of his trousers, but Deane leapt away from her as though she were made of fire.

"Enough of this, Lady Rathkenny," he nearly shouted at her. "Behave yourself like a woman of your station." He skated within inches of telling her that Chloe would never behave so vilely, and that Chloe wasn't the one who should be shunned for her scandalous behavior. "I am leaving now," he said instead. "Please tell my aunt and uncle that I was unwell and that I have decided to walk home."

"But—" Lady Rathkenny rose clumsily to her feet.

"Good evening, madam." Deane executed a crisp, formal bow, then strode out of the room.

Once he was in the hall, he dashed desperately away, looking for an escape. He had to find Chloe to explain the entire mess as quickly as possible. And after that, he needed to figure out how to speak to Fergus O'Shea immediately, before Lady Rathkenny found a way to twist her failures that evening into a sharper trap from which he wouldn't be able to escape.

CHAPTER 9

*C*hloe's patience for being shunted aside and treated as though she were unworthy was coming to a swift and decisive end. She'd tossed and turned all night, waiting for the proper time to call on Deane to ask about Shannon's assessment that he was about to be engaged to Lady Rathkenny. Then, when she'd waited as long as she could to ride her bicycle to Toome Hall to ask Deane for the true story, she'd been turned away by Hennessey, the Toomes' butler. And not nicely either.

Only when she had pedaled halfway down the Toomes' lane on her way home did she stop to wonder what could possibly have given a man like Hennessey the idea that he could treat her, the daughter of an earl, so shabbily.

"It isn't as though we dress in rags," Chloe complained to Shannon once she was home. "There are several titled gentlemen within the O'Shea family. Fergus is an earl, cousin Avery is an earl as well, and cousin Caelean is a viscount. And don't we have another viscount on one of the branches of the family tree?"

"Not another viscount," Shannon answered as she pored through the accounting books for her business. She glanced up and went on with, "There are several barons, though, on the more distant branches."

"Whatever the case," Chloe went on, shaking her head as she paced the room beside Shannon's desk, "what have I specifically done that makes people think they can speak down to me and treat me as though I am nothing?"

"Not a thing, dearest," Shannon said. "Some people feel the need to behave abominably toward others because they are unhappy with themselves."

"True," Chloe said. "But there must be something in the way I deport myself that signals I am to be treated as lesser." Shannon looked as though she were about to disagree, but Chloe cut her off with, "Well, I will not stand for it anymore. I am the daughter of an earl, I am a kind person, and I will not be cast aside like a fish that is too small. I will get to the bottom of things, and I will do it without being turned way."

Of course, within moments of knocking on the door of Loughguile Park, Chloe was turned away once again. The way that butler dismissed her without even asking her name didn't bode well for her chances of reaching Deane, but she refused to be deterred. If no one would help her reach the man she loved, she would just have to reach him herself.

She'd found the dining room purely by chance and managed to peek inside from the very bottom corner of one of the windows, praying no one would see her. Just as she'd suspected, the family was far too engaged with themselves and their special guests to bother looking out the window into the dark. The brightness of the dining room contrasted with the darkness of the October evening helped her concealment. She also considered it pure luck that Deane was seated at the end of the table, and that he did see her. As soon as their eyes met, she gestured for him to find a way to meet her. Not even Deane could turn her away, now that the bee was in her bonnet.

She wasn't surprised that he had to employ a ruse to get away from the supper table. She wasn't surprised that it took him a bit to find a room with an outside exit. She *was* surprised when Lady Rathkenny crept into the room several yards behind him, though.

"What does that odious woman want?" she muttered to herself, planting herself on the other side of the French doors, aware Deane could see her, but Lady Rathkenny couldn't.

Deane's conversation with Lady Rathkenny was muted to the point where Chloe couldn't hear the words they were speaking, although she could hear the tones of their voices.

"If that woman thinks she can sink her claws into

Deane now, she has another think coming," Chloe whispered to herself, attempting to ascertain the topic of the conversation through body language.

Lady Rathkenny seemed to either be making a desperate bid or to speed along whatever sort of proposal Deane might have intended to make. Deane looked flustered, which was a point in his favor, but the way his eyes popped when Lady Rathkenny slipped her gown off her shoulders had Chloe ready to leap through the glass to take him to task for being...well, for being a man.

The only thing that stopped her from taking action was Deane raising his voice enough for Chloe to make out, "Enough of this, Lady Rathkenny." He was frustrated with the vile woman, which was a point in Deane's favor, as far as Chloe was concerned. Deane went on, speaking to Lady Rathkenny in low, frank tones. Chloe only wished she could see Lady Rathkenny's face to know how the woman was taking his statements.

By the time Deane was finished, Chloe was finished as well. She backed away from the French doors and into the shadows, where no one could see her. As she turned when Deane left the room, intent on catching up to him at whatever other exit he found, Lady Rathkenny pivoted toward the window. Instead of rushing off, Chloe rocked back, curious to see what the woman might be thinking. Lady Rathkenny's expression was pinched with an unattractive combination of embarrassment, desperation, and determination.

It served her right, as far as Chloe was concerned.

She turned to head on to her meeting with Deane, but as she moved, she could have sworn Lady Rathkenny's head popped up a bit as she glanced out the window. Chloe prayed she was imagining things and hurried on, looking for some sort of back door.

"There you are," Deane's whisper came through the night a few seconds later.

Chloe could just make out his shadow as he marched around the corner of the house. She picked up her skirts and hurried to meet him.

"Would you mind telling me what the devil is going on here?" she hissed to him across the darkness, rushing up to him.

"I was about to ask you the same thing," he said.

They met in what appeared to be the corner of an herb garden of some sort, several yards away from what must have been a kitchen door.

"Shannon told me that you sent a telegraph to someone yesterday, saying that you planned to marry Lady Rathkenny by Christmas," Chloe whispered tightly, scowling at him.

There was just enough light for her to see Deane roll his eyes and press a hand to his forehead in a gesture of impatience. "I did send a telegram," he said in an irritated tone. "And it seems as though everyone standing in the post office yesterday overheard and misunderstood the message entirely."

A modicum of the tension Chloe had been carrying since Shannon's report the day before faded. "So you are not engaged to Lady Rathkenny?" she asked, taking a step toward him.

"Chloe," he said, his mouth twitching into a faint grin. "Do you really think I would settle for a disagreeable woman like her when I have you?"

More of Chloe's anxiety melted, but she said, "To be honest, I don't know. That is to say, I thought I knew you as well as could be, in spite of the brevity of our acquaintance. But how could I—"

She was cut off as the kitchen door swung open and the scullery maid lugged a huge pot out to empty in the kitchen courtyard. Light from the kitchen flooded the area as she did so.

Deane grabbed Chloe's elbow and escorted her back the way she'd come, away from the kitchen activity and the light. As soon as they were in an undisturbed part of the garden again, Deane said, "I'm sorry, my dear. I know you have a litany of logical reasons not to trust me. I will admit, there is a mountain of circumstantial evidence that might suggest I am not trustworthy to begin with."

Chloe squirmed a bit, letting the gesture bring her physically closer to Deane. She rested a hand on the front of his dinner jacket, suddenly wondering if he were cold without his coat. "I will admit that all of the rumors gave me pause," she said, glancing up at him. "But you've been so very honest with me all along. I thought to myself that it would be unfair of me not to take you at your word. Nothing in your star chart suggests that you are a duplicitous sort. In fact, the influence of Capricorn in your—"

Another creak, like a door opening, sounded toward the house. Chloe tensed, and Deane closed his arms around her as Lady Rathkenny's voice called out, "Hello? Is somebody out there?"

Chloe thanked Heaven for the darkness that enveloped her and Deane, and for a few well-placed shrubs. Deane was able to whisk her behind one at the corner of a long boxwood hedge that bordered a dormant flower garden.

"I'm certain I saw you out here, whomever you are," Lady Rathkenny said, sounding arrogant and imperious. "If you are a thief, you should know that I've alerted my father's butler to search the premises. The police will be called."

"Good heavens, the police," Deane said with mock terror.

His antics brought Chloe close to laughing, which would have been disaster at that moment, all things considered. She had such a hard time keeping quiet that she had to move, racing along the boxwood hedge with Deane, to get as far away from Lady Rathkenny as she could.

The boxwood hedge ended in a gravel path that appeared to run from a terrace connected to one of the side of the Loughguiles' house, between two gardens, and on to what Chloe could barely make out as some sort of tiny greenhouse or garden shed or guard house closer to the road. She'd left her bicycle just beyond the gate at the end of the drive, and with a quick tug on Deane's sleeve she stepped onto the path.

"Wait." Deane held her back, sweeping her into his arms again at the edge of the path.

"Oh," Chloe said, disappointment echoing in her voice. "Do you want to go back to the supper party?"

"Absolutely not," Deane whispered, pulling her close. "I want to explain what happened."

"Go on," Chloe said, her heart speeding up in anticipation.

Deane let out a frustrated sigh and brushed a strand of hair back from her forehead. "My aunt and Lady Loughguile arranged this blasted evening, of course," he said. "I wanted no part of it, but as usual, I was dragged here. The entire Loughguile family seems to be operating under the same misconception as your sister. In truth, I am not engaged to Lady Rathkenny, and I would rather live out the rest of my existence as a stoker shoveling coal in the boiler room of a steamship headed to Tasmania than as that woman's husband."

"I'm so relieved to hear that," Chloe breathed out. "Not the bit about being a stoker. That must be a hard life. Although Tasmania would be an exciting adventure."

Deane grinned down at her as though she'd said something wonderful. "You're the only woman I could imagine spending the rest of my life with," he said.

"Oh," Chloe gasped, her insides turning to butter.

She blinked and stiffened. "What about the telegram, then?"

Deane opened his mouth to answer, but before he could, one of the doors leading out to the terrace opened and Lord Loughguile stumbled out. He took a few unsteady steps across the flagstones, then proceeded to double over and vomit noisily.

"That man is a menace," Deane growled. He grabbed Chloe's hand and whisked her off down the path as Lord Loughguile heaved up more of his supper.

"Shouldn't we have a care to be quiet on this gravel?" Chloe whispered, anxious to get as far away from the house as possible.

"I don't think Lord Loughguile is going to notice or care," Deane murmured back.

All the same, they sped all the way down the path to the outbuilding—which turned out to be a decorative garden shed. The ornate door was unlocked, so they slipped inside. The structure had windows in the other three walls, all of which had wide windowsills, perhaps a little to high for sitting, but perfect for leaning against or for potted plants. They let in enough light that Chloe could make out Deane's features when he turned to her.

"I dare anyone to disturb us in here," he said, speaking at a normal volume. "I dare anyone to disturb us at all."

He surprised her by sliding his arms around her and slanting his mouth over hers for a passionate kiss. Chloe adored Deane's kisses, but in that moment, he startled her so much that she yelped and failed to kiss him back properly.

"Are you certain this is wise?" she asked in a high, breathless voice.

"I'm not certain anything I do could be considered wise," Deane laughed. "But this is the only thing I can think of to demonstrate how wrong everything your sister told you is and how badly everyone has misunderstood what they think they overheard at the post office."

He kissed her again, and Chloe warmed even more to him. She slid her hands under the hem of his dinner jacket so that she could spread them across his sides as she kissed him back. Everything about Deane radiated love and honesty. She felt like a fool for entertaining so much as a shred of a doubt in him.

"But wait," she said breathlessly, stopping their kiss. "What was the telegram about, then? Shannon seemed to think it most definitely had to do with a Christmas wedding."

Deane laughed quietly, grinning down at her. "I promised my sister, Victoria, that when I found the right bride, I would tell her first. Victoria and I are very close, even though she's ten years older than I am, and I owed it to her to keep my promise."

Chloe's heart squeezed in her chest. "That might be the loveliest thing I've heard all day," she sighed.

He looked mildly surprised. "You don't mind?" he asked. "Because it has delayed me speaking to your brother."

He was apologizing to her, but the substance of his apology sent pure joy blossoming through Chloe. Because he intended to speak to Fergus about marrying her.

"I don't mind one bit," she said, her voice so full of emotion that she could hardly contain it. "I could wait an eternity for you. But I hope I don't have to."

"My darling," Deane sighed, surging into her for another kiss. "You won't have to wait at all."

His kiss was so ardent and so beautiful that Chloe wondered how she could ever have doubted him to begin with. Rumors were only pale imitations of the way people truly were, and words were only stories. It was action and kisses that told the truth, and the way Deane's mouth devoured hers, the way his hands roved up her sides, unbuttoning her coat so that he could feel her heat and caress her, said everything she needed to know.

"I love you, my darling Gemini," Deane murmured against her mouth, pulling her flush against him.

Chloe sighed with joy and pleasure. "And I love you, even though you're a Scorpio."

Deane laughed, but the humor of the moment only made it more passionate. His kisses grew possessive and deep, and Chloe didn't want them to stop. Ever. So much so that she went to work unbuttoning his dinner jacket and waistcoat, then tugged his shirt out of his trousers so that he could feel the heat of his skin against her palms.

From there, things spiraled out of control in no time at all. Their kisses turned fiery, and their hands pulled at clothing and groped at skin. A faint voice at the back of Chloe's mind warned her they were careening toward something dangerous, but it was too exciting for her to want to stop. Particularly when she brazenly unfastened Deane's trousers so that she could caress his stiff and proud prick.

"Dear God, Chloe, I want you," he panted raggedly against her ear, then kissed his way down her neck, unbuttoning her high-collared shirt as he did so that he could kiss more of her.

"I'm yours," she moaned. She blinked, gasping for breath, and looked up at him. "Can we do what we did yesterday in here?"

His eyes widened, then narrowed. "We can, and you won't even have to undress, if you're willing."

"I am more than willing," she said with absolute seriousness.

Deane's eyes lit with mirth and lust, and he reached for her skirt, tugging it up to expose her legs. "I've done all sorts of wicked things before, but this might just be the wickedest of all," he purred.

"I already love it," Chloe said, matching his tone and intensity.

As soon as he had her skirts and petticoats gathered around her waist, he lifted her to one of the windowsills, resting her bum on the edge. They might have been too high for sitting, but they were the perfect height for other things. Chloe leaned back against the window, and when Deane pushed her knees far apart and slipped his fingers through the split in her drawers to test her readiness, she moaned with pleasure and gripped the window frame.

"You're so wet," he growled, moving against her. He kissed her neck while stroking and teasing the part of her that ached for him.

"It's because I want you," she panted, spreading her legs farther. "Oh, that feels so good. I feel like I'm going to—"

He didn't give her a chance to finish. His hands disappeared for a moment as he fiddled with his trousers. A heartbeat later, she felt him hot and hard against her, then pushing firmly inside of her. It felt so amazingly good that she cried out with joy and arched into him.

"You're so free with yourself," he gasped, positioning her hips just so and digging his fingertips in for purchase. "I cannot get enough of you."

A moment later, Chloe was completely incapable of speech as he thrust into her repeatedly. It was wicked and beautiful, and as soon as he had her angled perfectly against the window and found the right balance and purchase for himself, he moved in her so commandingly that her body couldn't help but sing and throb and burst into the most powerful orgasm she'd ever had. It went on and on as she cried out with carnal joy in time to his thrusts, throwing her head back against the window and likely leaving indents in the wood as her fingernails dug into the window frame.

Deane was vocal in his appreciation of her as well, which Chloe loved. The heat and tension of his body poured off of him in the most beautiful way, and the sounds he made, coupled with the intensity in his body as he spilled himself into her, was one of the most perfect things she'd ever experienced.

It was as fast and powerful as lightning, and even when it was over, it was as though they'd both been struck. Chloe had her legs locked around Deane's waist, and as he sagged against her and the window, both of them fighting to catch their breaths, she didn't want to let him go. He felt too right inside of her, filling her, and she dreaded the moment when they would no longer be joined, even if that moment had to come.

"I love you," Deane sighed. "You are astounding to me."

"And you are—"

A thump and shuffling of gravel outside of the shed cut off Chloe's words, ending her endearment with a gasp instead. Deane stiffened, then pulled out and away from her, drawing her with him as he did.

"Do you see anyone outside?" Chloe whispered.

Deane craned his neck to look around her. "I don't think I do. It could have been the wind, or a dog, or some other creature."

"It could have been a person," Chloe whispered even quieter.

Deane glanced warily to her and nodded. "Don't worry," he said, kissing her and helping her to put herself in order. "If we were seen, I will not forsake you."

"I knew you wouldn't," she told him with a smile, helping him to dress again as well.

"All the same, I should speak to your brother as soon as possible," Deane went on.

"He and Henrietta have gone to Belfast on business for a few days," Chloe winced. Immediately, she brightened. "But they'll be back for Marie and Christian's luncheon in two days. Things won't spin out of control in two days, will they?"

"I don't think so," Deane said, kissing her again as they finished straightening themselves. "Two days is nothing."

"Come to Kilrea Manor in two days." Chloe kissed him back. "We'll resolve everything there."

"We will," Deane said, giving her one long, final kiss. "And once it's resolved we'll make those rumors everyone has spread about a Christmas wedding into a reality."

CHAPTER 10

Two mornings later, Deane awoke brimming with excitement and ready to speak to Lord Fergus O'Shea so that he could ask the most important question of his life. He was well aware of how foolish he and Chloe had been at Loughguile Park, but he just hadn't been able to help himself. Which, he admitted, was a very serious weakness of his. Chloe had looked beautiful and righteous in her anger of what was, fortunately, a misunderstanding, the outbuilding had been perfectly placed for wickedness, and the thrill of the moment had suspended his judgement. It was a good thing on several levels for Deane to speak to Lord O'Shea so that he and Chloe could be married in due haste, because he couldn't guarantee that he wouldn't commit the same glorious sin again, over and over, if given half a chance.

His feet and heart were light as he nearly danced

down the stairs of Toome Hall so that he could be on his way to the luncheon at Kilrea Manor. He was hours too early, but he didn't care. Arriving early would merely give him a chance to make a good impression on Chloe's sister and brother-in-law.

"And where do you think you're going in such a rush?" his aunt caught him at the bottom of the stairs, before he could cross the hall to where Hennessey was holding both the door and his coat. Hennessey closed the door in a movement that held far too much foreboding for Deane's liking.

"I have an invitation to luncheon at Lord Kilrea's house," Deane informed his aunt. She was going to learn the truth of things soon, so why not now?

Lady Toome narrowed her eyes. "You have no such thing," she said.

Deane blinked, uncertain whether she was accusing him of something or attempting to change his plans. "I beg your pardon?"

To his utter surprise, Lady Toome broke into a sly grin. "You cannot hide the truth from me," she said. "You, my dear boy, are flying off to meet your secret lover."

Deane was utterly flummoxed by the woman's boldness in suggesting such a thing and her apparent delight in it. "I'm not," he said carefully. "Not precisely, that is. I am, indeed, invited to luncheon at Lord Kilrea's house, because Lord Fergus O'Shea will be there." He paused, then added significantly, "And his sister, Lady Chloe."

Lady Toome's mischievous expression dropped into a

look of shock and panic. "What does that ninny have to do with anything? Lady Rathkenny is the one you are marrying."

Deane sighed and pressed his fingertips to his temples to fight off the ongoing headache his aunt represented. "Dear Aunt Ermengarde, for the dozenth time, I am no more interested in marrying Lady Rathkenny than I am in marrying Hennessey over there." He flung his arm out toward the butler. "I find Lady Rathkenny to be conniving, immodest, and sharp. I could never find the least bit of happiness with her, and even though it is devilishly unfashionable of me, I wish only to marry a woman with whom I could be happy, as my beloved parents were happy with each other."

"Happiness has nothing to do with marriage," Lady Toome said with a scowl, growing angrier by the moment. "Do you think I am happy with your uncle?"

"Er, well...."

"I knew you were a rake and a cad, but I had no idea you would ruin a woman the way you have ruined Lady Rathkenny and then refuse to marry her," his aunt went on.

Again, Deane had no idea what was going on. "I have not ruined Lady Rathkenny in any way," he said.

His aunt's eyes went wide. "There are rumors circulating amongst certain circles that you were spotted in an outbuilding of Loughguile Park *in a scandalous situation with a woman*," she lowered her voice to deliver the last bit of her sentence.

Deane was instantly mortified. The sounds he and Chloe had heard the other night must have been human after all. But in spite of the way he heated with embarrassment, inside and out, he said, "You must be mistaken. Rumors rarely have substance behind them, as I well know. Now, if you will excuse me, I am expected at Kilrea Manor."

He walked on toward the door, but his aunt called after him, "But you cannot!"

"Cannot accept an invitation to dine with an earl?" Deane asked as he took his coat from Hennessey.

"You cannot ally yourself with that ridiculous, wicked O'Shea family," Lady Toome insisted, hurrying after him.

Deane was at the end of his tether. "I can, madam, and I will. And there is nothing you can do to stop me. Now, if you will excuse me."

He shook his head at his aunt and strode out the door. It was outlandish that his aunt thought she could steer the course of his future and determine whom he would marry. Her machinations were likely designed to improve her standing in her community for a season, but any decision Deane made about a wife would be with him for the rest of his life. He would have regretted his decision to take Lady Toome up on her offer of assisting him in finding a bride and clearing his reputation if it hadn't led him to Chloe.

Those thoughts ground away in him as he rounded the side of Toome Hall, heading toward the stables. He'd sent word to the stablemaster to have a horse ready for him before coming downstairs, but as he approached the stable, one of the footmen dashed into the courtyard ahead of him, and as Deane came within view of the stable door, he spotted the young man leaping onto the only saddled horse at the ready.

"Oy! Where do you think you're going?" the stable master shouted at the lad as he nudged the horse into a run straight out of the stables. Deane had to jump out of the way as the horse tore past him and out through the courtyard to the road. "I'm so sorry, Your Grace," the stable master said as soon as Deane continued on. "That was the only mount we had ready. I don't know what possessed the boy. I'll have another mount saddled for you as quickly as possible."

As quickly as possible turned out to be another twenty minutes, which Deane took as no surprise. Even after that, there was a further delay in riding the horse out of the courtyard as a few of the maids had upset a cart near the only exit wide enough for a horse to pass though. They both looked embarrassed and anxious about the predicament and were, suspiciously, no help at all in cleaning up the mess and righting the cart. It was clearly a ploy to delay him from setting out, though Deane couldn't figure out what use his aunt must have thought it would be to prevent him from reaching Kilrea Manor sooner rather than later.

Once the cart was uprighted and Deane was able to head out across the countryside, he nudged his horse into a gallop, anxious about what might be going on without his knowledge. It was somehow unsurprising to him that he was delayed further when his horse threw a shoe within sight of Kilrea Manor. That forced him to stop and walk the rest of the way to avoid laming the horse.

The answer to his puzzlement over his delay seemed to be answered as he drew near to the grand manor house and was suddenly passed by an entire line of speeding carriages. Four of them, to be exact. One belonged to his uncle, and in another he was certain he spotted Lady Loughguile.

"Good lord, what now?" Deane grumbled as he walked the rest of the way up to Kilrea Manor.

He was met at the front of the house by a butler who was in a tizzy and a stable hand who was willing to take his horse and see that its shoe was fixed. The butler actually seemed relieved to see Deane and stepped forward to greet him.

"Many apologies, Your Grace," he said. "It seems as though Lord and Lady Kilrea have quite a few unexpected and uninvited guests for luncheon. I have never seen such a thing in all my years. I did my utmost to deny them entrance, but there were simply too many of them, and gentry among them."

"I'm afraid whatever this is, it is my fault," Deane apologized to the butler. "I will see if I can get to the bottom of the matter." They walked into the house, and Deane thought to ask, "Is Lord O'Shea here yet?"

"Yes, Your Grace," the butler said. "The entire family is here."

That much, at least, was a relief.

Or so Deane thought until he was shown into a large parlor that was packed to the gills with confused and agitated men and women. Deane knew Chloe and her brother and her sister Shannon, of course. He was less familiar with Lord and Lady Boleran, but knew them from their recent wedding. He'd only briefly met Lord and Lady Kilrea at the wedding, which was no surprise, considering Lady Kilrea's happy condition. That advanced condition was precisely why it was startling to find the woman attempting to play hostess to Lord and Lady Toome, Lord and Lady Loughguile, Lady Rathkenny, and, most surprisingly of all, over half a dozen other assorted ladies, most of whom, like Lady Alison, Lady Morrison, and Lady Eveline, Deane recognized as friends of Lady Rathkenny's.

"What the devil is going on here?" Deane asked, glancing first to Chloe with an almost apologetic look, then to his aunt, and finally, to Lady Rathkenny.

"I would very much like to know the same thing," Lord Kilrea asked, as though he had already been in the middle of demanding answers before Deane arrived.

Chloe started across the room to Deane, but Lady Toome stepped into her way to stop her.

"We were interrupted in the middle of a pleasant morning of relaxation," Lord Loughguile answered, as if he, too, didn't have the slightest idea what was going on.

"My dear Teresa and my lovely daughter Vanessa were hosting a morning meeting of their aide society—and likely gossiping away, as you know these sly things do," he added, elbowing Lord Kilrea with an inappropriate wink, "when some lad from Toome Hall comes galloping up to the house, saying we were all needed at Kilrea Manor immediately on a matter of life and death."

Deane scowled at his aunt. She'd sent for reinforcements, though for what, exactly, he wasn't certain. He rather dreaded the answer.

"There must be some mistake," Lord Kilrea said. "I have no need for extra company this morning. In fact, we were about to have an important, family luncheon. Therefore, I must ask you all to go."

"Not before certain rumors of a salacious nature are addressed," Lady Toome said, grabbing Chloe's wrist and holding her back a second time as she tried to head across the room to Deane.

"Lady Toome, I must ask you to unhand me," Chloe said with a frown. Deane was impressed that she didn't yank out of his aunt's grip and then turn and smack the woman.

"It has come to our attention that the Duke of Blackburn was seen the night before last in an outbuilding on our property destroying the virtue of a young woman," Lady Loughguile blurted, then clapped a hand to her mouth, as though she couldn't believe what she had said.

The gaggle of young ladies that stood clustered around Lady Rathkenny gasped and looked horrified.

They also glanced to Deane with excited looks, as though he were an object of fascination and desire.

Deane let out a sigh, his shoulders dropping. "I will admit—" he began, but stopped abruptly when he spotted Lord Kilrea shaking his head, his eyes wide with warning. Though Deane had no idea what the man was attempting to tell him, he changed his tactics. "I will admit that I was at Loughguile Park for supper the night before last, and I will admit that certain aspects of my reputation might lend one to think I was involved in whatever accusations are being made, but—"

"It was me!" Lady Rathkenny burst out with a sudden fit of emotion that was worthy of the most accomplished actress. She swept forward, taking up a position in the center of the room. "I confess, the lady in question, the one whose honor and purity were sacrificed on the altar of love with His Grace the other night, was me."

Again, Lady Rathkenny's Greek chorus of friends gasped, exchanging wide-eyed looks with each other. Deane couldn't quite determine if the young ladies were genuinely shocked, or whether they were all part of some premeditated plan. He didn't think they were complicit in his aunt's scheme.

Though now he wondered if it was his aunt's scheme alone. Everything suddenly made perfect sense. The rumors were already circulating because he and Chloe truly had been spotted making love in the outbuilding, but Lady Rathkenny had grabbed what she must have seen as a foolproof plan to trap him into marriage once and for all. Confessing that she was the woman Deane had been with was a massive risk that would grievously damage her reputation, but only in Ireland. She would come out of the scandal a duchess, and in her mind, she would never have to return to the scene of the scandal again. Bringing her friends as witnesses to the confession was her way of trapping Deane even further, because Lady Rathkenny must have believed that, in order to deny her, he would have to destroy Chloe's reputation entirely. The harpy was gambling that he would give in to a marriage trap in order to save the woman he loved.

Well, Lady Rathkenny was wrong. There had to be another way out of the trap.

"I have no idea what you are talking about, Lady Rathkenny," Deane said, pulling himself to his full height and frowning at her. "At no point have I ever been alone with you, and I most certainly would not engage in the sort of behavior with you that you are accusing me of."

"Are you denying that you were at our home the other evening?" Lady Loughguile asked, looking primed to be offended.

"I am not denying it," Deane said. He glanced desperately to Chloe, praying she wouldn't do herself a harm by confessing to being his paramour that night.

"And are you denying that you left supper early, without your uncle and I?" Lady Toome asked.

"I will not deny that either. I choked on my pudding and had to excuse myself to take care of the matter," he explained to the Greek chorus of feminine judges, hoping they would draw their own conclusions and imagine he'd been ill.

"And will the rest of you confirm that I left the dining room only a few moments after the Duke of Blackburn did?" Lady Rathkenny said, unable to hide her triumphant grin and the predatory sparkle in her eyes as she glanced to Deane.

"You did," Lady Toome said with exaggerated feeling, as if only just drawing salacious conclusions. "You most certainly did."

"There is your proof, then," Lady Rathkenny said. She resumed her overly dramatic demeanor with a sigh and shifted into a falsely contrite pose. "I let love get the better of me. I have betrayed my family and my virtue by allowing myself to be led astray. But I did it with the understanding that I would not be forsaken, that His Grace held me in high enough regard to do the honorable thing and make this unfortunate lapse of moral judgement into a temporary one instead of a lifelong sorrow."

"You bounder!" Lord Loughguile bellowed, staring at Deane in offense. "And after I invited you into my home. I should have heeded the warnings about your character and kept you as far away from my family as possible."

Deane sighed and pressed his fingertips to his temples in a gesture that was becoming entirely too familiar. He was certain Lord Loughguile wasn't a part of the ladies' machinations, but the man wasn't helping the situation one bit.

"Lord Loughguile," he said, trying to sound apologetic, but actually sounding weary, "I can assure you that this is all a misunderstanding. I would never importune your daughter in such a way. I don't even like her."

"Darling, how dare you?" Lady Rathkenny gasped. She started toward Deane. "We should be married at once and—"

"You will marry him over my dead body," Chloe snapped, finally able to get away from Lady Toome before she was grabbed and restrained again. "I will not allow a vicious harpy such as you to ruin the life of a dear, kind, generous man." She marched right up to Deane's side, grasping his arm. "If you must know, I am the one who—"

"I think we've all had just about enough of this," Lord O'Shea snapped, rolling his wheelchair into the center of the room.

Whether it was the man's commanding manner or the awkwardness that Lady Rathkenny and her parents and minions must have felt over a man in a wheelchair taking center stage in the drama, no one spoke up to contradict him.

"Lord Loughguile, Lord Toome," Lord O'Shea went on, addressing the gentlemen in the opposing camp, even though Lord Toome had remained silent and baffled through the entire scene, "if you will allow me a moment in private to speak with my family and sort out this mess, I would greatly appreciate it."

"That would, er, be just fine, um, I believe," Lord Toome said, blinking rapidly and shrugging.

"Thank you," Fergus said, wheeling his chair on toward the hall. "Anyone who is related to me or wishes to be related to me, in the music room, now."

The command was given so firmly—and with a hint of humor glittering in Lord O'Shea's one eye—that Deane couldn't help but shuffle out of the parlor and down the hall to the music room, along with more than half of the odd party, leaving the others to stew in restless anticipation.

CHAPTER 11

As soon as they left the parlor and started down the hall to the music room, Deane had the sense that even though the O'Shea family was considered wicked and undesirable by certain people in high society, they were a family that supported each other, no matter what the circumstances.

"Would somebody like to explain to me what in the name of all that is good and holy is going on here?" Lord O'Shea said as soon as they were all safely within the music room, spread out in a circle, almost like a grand council, convened to solve all of the world's problems.

Lady Henrietta O'Shea stood by the side of her husband's wheelchair with a hand on his shoulder. Lord Kilrea helped his pregnant wife to a seat on the sofa. Lady Boleran had a seat beside her while Lord Boleran took up a position behind her, hovering protectively.

Lady Shannon took a seat in one of the room's overstuffed chairs, looking like a mythical queen on a throne. That left Deane standing where he was, Chloe still holding his arm, as though claiming him as her own.

"It's simple, really, Fergus," Chloe said, seemingly a thousand times more comfortable in front of the jury of her family than Deane had ever seen her in the company of others. "I love Deane—that is, the Duke of Blackburn—and he loves me, and he came here to ask you a question, Fergus." Her eyes glittered with joy and love as she glanced from Deane to her brother and back again.

"Is that so?" Lord O'Shea asked Deane, narrowing his one eye. "You've come here today to ask for my sister's hand?"

"I have," Deane answered.

It was a simple answer, but it sent a ripple of surprise through the room. Lord O'Shea sat a bit straighter in his chair, Lady Shannon grinned from ear to ear, and Lord Boleran and Lord Kilrea exchanged shocked looks.

"I told you," Lady Boleran said to her husband. "You owe me twenty pounds."

"Colleen!" Chloe exclaimed. "Were you and your groom betting on whether His Grace would propose to me?"

"We were," Lady Boleran said, "And I win. I'll win an additional twenty pounds if the two of you have already—" She gestured between Deane and Chloe.

"Does this mean you didn't think he would propose?"

Chloe asked Lord Boleran with an adorable amount of impertinence in her tilted-up chin. She blushed pink and added, "And yes, you owe Colleen another twenty pounds. Or forty, depending on how you choose to see the situation."

Colleen snorted into laughter, covering her mouth.

"It isn't that I didn't think Blackburn is fond of you," Lord Boleran said, squirming where he stood, as if the last thing he wanted to be conversing about was his sister-in-law's love life.

"I am excessively fond of Lady Chloe," Deane said, wanting to improve the moral tone of the conversation and make no secret of his feelings for Chloe. "She is the only woman I've met so far in Ireland who has treated me as a person and a man rather than a duke and a point of gossip." He smiled at Chloe with all the love in his heart. "I have confessed all of my secrets to her, because Chloe is ridiculously easy to confess everything to, and she has forgiven me. She has really and truly forgiven me for my mistakes and my indiscretions rather than holding them against me or treating them as something titillating." He glanced back to the others, especially Lord O'Shea. "I cannot tell you how embarrassed I am over what I allowed to happen over the summer."

"You didn't *allow* it to happen," Chloe corrected him. "You were taken advantage of in your grief by women who should have known better."

That statement seemed to stun the others.

"Taken advantage of?" Lord O'Shea asked.

Deane's face went hot, and he had to fight the sheep-ishness that clenched his gut. Lord O'Shea was of an age with him, and by anyone else's measure, the man ranked lower, but Deane felt as though he was under scrutiny by an older and wiser man. He would soon be family, though, if Deane had his way.

"I was grieving the loss of my parents and allowed the offer of affection to turn my head," he said, wanting to dwell on it as little as possible. "Doing so earned me a reputation that is as far from my natural character as could be."

"Grief can do strange things to us," Lord Kilrea said, taking his wife's hand and squeezing it. "As I know too well."

"But everything was made right in the end," Lady Kilrea said, leaning in to kiss her husband lightly. Deane knew he was in the inner circle of the family after that tender gesture.

"Everything will be made right in the end for us as well," Chloe went on, facing her family with a show of strength. "I'm sure you have all guessed that it was not Lady Rathkenny in the outbuilding with His Grace the other night, it was me."

If Deane had been eating or drinking something, he would have choked again. Chloe's admission was so bald and so easily delivered that he could hardly believe he'd heard her confess something so intimate to her family.

Even more surprising, none of them reacted as though the world were coming to an end.

"That goes without saying," Lady Shannon said, though she shook her head somewhat. "I would have locked you in your bedroom if I'd known what you were planning that night."

"In Lady Chloe's defense," Deane said, feeling as though he needed to defend her, but also feeling as if he had no idea what sort of standards of judgement the O'Shea family had, "nothing that happened that night was planned."

"It's true," Chloe said, head lowered slightly. "I merely went to Loughguile Park to see if I could ascertain whether the things Shannon reported to me were true or not."

"And why did you go to Loughguile Park specifically instead of merely going to Toome Hall, where the man is staying?" Fergus asked, the eyebrow above his patch lifting.

"Because I was turned away when I went to Toome Hall earlier in the day," Chloe said.

"For which I am genuinely sorry," Deane said. "My aunt has it in her mind that I should marry Lady Rathkenny, regardless of how I feel about the matter."

"I see." Lord O'Shea rubbed his chin. "So what we are faced with here is a plot to marry Blackburn off against his will to a woman he doesn't care for."

Deane's brow shot up. "Yes, that is the situation." What surprised him was the calculated look that came over Lord O'Shea and, indeed, the rest of the family. They seemed to be treating the situation not as a major scandal that could rock the family's standing even further, but as an opportunity for mischief.

"Blackburn could simply refuse to marry Lady Rathkenny," Lord Boleran pointed out. "No one is going to force him to the altar with a pistol at his back."

"I wouldn't put it past my aunt," Deane said with a wary look.

"Yes, simply refusing to walk down any aisles would be the easy way out of things," Lady O'Shea said, though she wore the sort of grin that indicated that wasn't the way the O'Shea family handled their problems.

"Before we go on," Deane said, taking a step toward Lord O'Shea, "I feel there is something vital that needs to be said first, or rather, asked."

"Go on," Lord O'Shea said with a lopsided smile that somehow smacked of victory. He glanced to Chloe and winked, as though he'd gotten the better of her in an ongoing game at last.

"Lord O'Shea," Deane said, clearing his throat, "it would be a great honor to me if you would allow me the pleasure of taking Lady Chloe as my wife."

"I grant you that honor enthusiastically," Lord O'Shea said. "Take her, she's yours. Get the mischievous, stary-eyed little minx out of my house."

Chloe laughed for joy, but immediately stopped with what sounded like a hiccup and said, "Wait one moment, Fergus. Didn't you try to tell me, and not that long ago, that there was no possible way a duke would ever agree to marry me?"

Deane's brow shot up. "Blasphemy," he said. "Of course, I would want to marry you."

Lord O'Shea chuckled. "What I said was that I wouldn't be able to fix it if you got yourself into trouble, young lady. I didn't know love was involved. Love makes everything possible, even English dukes wanting to marry silly, sweet, astrologically-minded, Irish lasses."

"Hear, hear," Lady Shannon said, thumping the arm of her chair.

"But we still have the problem of Lady Rathkenny to solve," Lord Kilrea said. "And her band of witnesses who will be out for blood if they think Blackburn here has thrown her over after ruining her."

"She wasn't even the one in the outbuilding with Deane, though," Chloe sighed.

"Mistaken identities, illicit acts taking place in windows in the night, false accusations made by twisting the truth," Lady Kilrea said, excitement in her eyes. "It's almost like the plot for *Much Ado About Nothing*."

"Oh, yes it is," Lady Boleran said, perhaps a bit too excited. "When Don John made everyone think he was with Hero when, in fact, it was the maid."

"Yes, that seems to be exactly which script Lady Rathkenny is using to twist the situation to her own advantage," Lady O'Shea said.

"I won't let it happen," Chloe said. "Lady Rathkenny is vile, and I—"

She was cut off by the appearance of Lady Toome in

the doorway of the music room, Kilrea's flustered butler by her side.

"I told her you were not to be disturbed, my lord, but once again, she insisted," the poor man sighed.

"Not to worry, Cavanaugh," Lord Kilrea said.

"I will take care of this," Deane said, nodding to Lord O'Shea, smiling at Chloe, then turning to scowl at his aunt.

He marched out into the hall, intending to goose-step his aunt back to the parlor. He was surprised to find Lady Rathkenny waiting halfway down the hall, as if she had sent Lady Toome to do her bidding. The one bit of relief Deane found in the arrangement was that Lady Rathkenny was too far down the hall to have overheard a word of what had been said in the music room. She didn't look as though she would have cared one way or another. The woman radiated determination as Deane and Lady Toome walked down the hall to meet her.

"I have had enough of this prevaricating," Lady Rathkenny hissed, as though she were the one who had been taken advantage of in the situation. "I have risked everything, put my reputation on the line, and I will get what I want."

Deane gaped at her as he came to within a few feet of her. He kept his voice low so that no one in the parlor would over hear and said, "Any damage that has occurred to your reputation, Lady Rathkenny, any risk you have taken, is entirely of your own doing. At no point have I indicated in any way that I wish to marry you or so much as be associated with you."

"Then you are a fool," she snapped. "I am far and away the best match for you. I am the only woman you have been introduced to who is equal to the task of being your duchess. *I* am the one with ambition. *I* am the one with talent and skill. *I* am the one who deserves that place in society." She poked her finger at her chest with each of her pronouncements.

"Madam, you are ambitious, I will give you that much and that much alone," Deane said. "But your character is sorely lacking. And you have mistaken my character entirely."

"You are a duke," she said with a restless, fluttering gesture. "What does it matter if you have character at all? You have money, you have position, and you have estates where I will be more than happy to live out my life entirely separate from you, if that is what you wish."

"You are failing to hear what I am attempting to tell you, madam," Deane went on, losing patience with the woman. "I do not wish to marry you, and I will not be trapped into it."

"*You* are not listening to what *we* have to tell you," Lady Toome said. "Lady Rathkenny is the perfect bride for you. I will not lose my chance to be applauded for making the match, or the chance to be consulted by society in future matchmaking endeavors, simply because you fancy a silly, salacious O'Shea."

Deane's eyes popped open. So there was his aunt's

motivation in pushing the match so hard. She wanted to make a place for herself as a society matchmaker. She likely thought there could be financial compensation involved in a position like that as well. He should have seen something of the like coming.

"I am terribly sorry to have thwarted your plans," Deane said, unable to keep the sarcasm out of his voice, even though he knew it was unkind, "but I am now engaged to marry Lady Chloe O'Shea, and that is what I fully intend to do."

"Oh, blast Lady Chloe O'Shea!" Lady Rathkenny shouted, likely loud enough for everyone in both the parlor and the music room to overhear. "I will not be thwarted by that insignificant little chit. Keep her as your mistress if you want, I don't care. If you get her with child, you can even claim that the brat is mine and keep it as your heir. Rathkenny never managed to get a brat of his own off of me anyhow, so it may end up being necessary. I could not care one bit. Just give me what is mine."

If there had been a shred of doubt in Deane's mind that Lady Rathkenny was the last woman on earth he could have married, that outburst would have settled it. "Lady Rathkenny, this conversation is over," he said, marching ahead of her to the parlor with every intention of telling her family and friends as much. He turned the corner into the room only to find everyone watching, as though they knew full well what sort of conversation had taken place in the hallway.

But Lord Loughguile, at the prompting of his wife,

stumbled forward and greeted Deane by taking his arm and leading him into the center of the room. "Ah, Blackburn. Am I to take it that a happy announcement needs to be made?" he asked, pink-faced and peeking desperately at his wife.

Lady Loughguile gestured furiously at the man, as if the situation could be resolved in their favor if he would just hurry up and get on with things.

"An announcement will be made," Deane said, his patience more than at an end, "but you will not be the one making it."

"Nonsense," Lady Rathkenny said, as desperate as ever, as she swept into the room. She tried to take Deane's arm, but he stepped away from her before she could sink her claws in. "Go ahead, Papa," she said, her smile far to wide to be anything other than pure panic, "tell everyone the happy news."

"I think not," Deane said. "Ladies and gentlemen," he said to the baffled group lingering around the edges of the parlor, looking as though they were attending some sort of melodrama, and that they had been seated directly on the stage, "I regret to inform you that there has been an egregious misunderstanding. The events of the other night—"

"There is no need for you to explain, Your Grace," Chloe said, bursting into the doorway as though it were the proscenium of a magnificent stage. She stepped into the room, allowing the rest of the combined force of the O'Shea family to crowd into the room behind her. Deane couldn't help but notice poorly-concealed grins and eyes sparkling with mirth from all of them. "There is no need to explain, Your Grace," Chloe repeated, holding up her arms, "because I have an explanation for everything. It is time for the truth to finally come out."

CHAPTER 12

The key to the entire ruse was *Much Ado About Nothing*. The moment Chloe had been reminded of the story, she knew exactly how to extricate Deane from Lady Rathkenny's claws and teach the woman a lesson about attempting to ensnare a husband against his will as well. She didn't consider herself the best actress of her sisters, but she was willing to give it a go.

"Yes," she said, arms raised, chin tilted up, rather enjoying the way everyone in the room was captivated by her, "I am here now to tell you the truth."

"And I suppose you are going to claim that you were the woman in the outbuilding with the Duke of Blackburn?" Lady Rathkenny sniffed as though she'd seen the ploy coming a mile away, but she looked desperately anxious all the same. "It would be a ridiculous story," she went on, "and a decidedly convenient way to trap a man who could never marry you into matrimony." She laughed, but the sound was brittle and sharp.

Some of her friends attempted to laugh with her, but most of them were deeply confused.

Chloe tried to hide her smile of victory, but she simply couldn't do it. "I will confess," she sighed, "I was not the lady in the outbuilding with His Grace."

Both Deane and Lady Rathkenny blinked in surprise. Lady Rathkenny burst into a smile, as though she'd won at last. Deane opened his mouth as if to contradict Chloe, looking a bit desperate himself, but Chloe shook her head subtly at him, begging for patience. Deane shut his mouth again, but looked as though he would intervene in a moment if things went wrong and he was in danger of being forced to marry Lady Rathkenny.

"You see?" Lady Rathkenny demanded of her audience, turning to look at each one of them as though she'd conquered an empire instead of merely admitting to a salacious dalliance. "*I* was the lady in the outbuilding that night. *I* was the one whose honor was ruined. *I* am the one who demands to have the situation made right." She turned to Deane. "You cannot be such a cad that you would refuse to marry the woman whom you have admitted to ruining in front of all these witnesses."

"I have admitted to no such thing," Deane said, staring hard at Chloe.

"It is true," Chloe said, practically quivering on the inside as her plan reached its apex. "You have admitted to being the lady in the outbuilding that night," Chloe said one more time, digging Lady Rathkenny's hole deeper.

"I have, and I was," Lady Rathkenny said, bringing along her own shovel.

"But it was not the Duke of Blackburn in the outbuilding with you," she said with a dramatic flourish, loving every moment of her speech.

Right on cue, all of Lady Rathkenny's friends, and even Lady Loughguile, gasped.

"It was not the Duke of Blackburn in the outbuilding with you," Chloe repeated, figuring the more times her audience heard it, the better the whole ruse would turn out, "because His Grace was at Dunegard Castle, speaking to my brother, Lord Fergus O'Shea, asking for my hand in marriage."

"It's true," Fergus spoke up, corroborating her story. "Blackburn spent the evening at Dunegard Castle, where I consented to let him marry my miscreant little sister." Fergus couldn't hide his amusement at the whole scene, although his grin, combined with his eyepatch, made him look like a wicked brigand.

"No!" Lady Rathkenny shouted, her eyes going wide in horror. "That isn't true. It most certainly is not true."

"She's right," Lady Toome said, her cheeks splashed with color and her eyes wide with horror as all of her neat plans unfurled. "My nephew was at Loughguile Park that night. We all saw him." She gestured to Lord and Lady Loughguile.

Finally, Deane's mouth twitched into a smile as he

caught on to the plan. "As you will recall, dear aunt," he said, drawing himself up to his full height and stepping from the side of the parlor that contained his aunt and uncle, the Loughguiles, Lady Rathkenny, and her friends, "I left the supper table early, as I was choking. I was able to clear my throat immediately, however, and rather than return to the dining room or the company of Loughguile Park, I departed immediately for Dunegard Castle."

"You did not," Lady Rathkenny said, her face splotched red. "We spoke in the winter parlor moments later. You know we did."

Deane pretended to be confused. "We did not, my lady." It was an actual lie, for a change.

"We did, we did," Lady Rathkenny insisted, stomping her foot.

"B-but I thought you said that you had an assignation with the duke in an outbuilding," Lady Alison spoke up, serving as the mouthpiece for all of the ladies that had been dragged to Kilrea Manor to serve as witnesses. "Now you're saying it was the parlor?"

"It was the parlor and the outbuilding," Lady Rathkenny whined.

"But why begin an assignation in a parlor and end it in an outbuilding?" Lady Morrison asked, narrowing her eyes at Lady Rathkenny.

"Something is very wrong here," Lady Eveline said, crossing her arms and frowning.

"Yes, yes it is," Lady Rathkenny said, making one last, desperate plea. "I demand you tell them that I was the one in the outbuilding with you that night and that you will marry me," she said to Deane.

"I cannot, madam," Deane said with a shrug and a shake of his head. "As you have heard, I departed Loughguile Park for Dunegard Castle, as Lord O'Shea has confirmed."

"I will confirm it as well," Henrietta said. "His Grace spoke to me also."

"And me," Shannon added, her eyes alight with mirth.

"My beautiful bride and I were there as well," Lord Boleran said as Colleen nodded.

"So you see?" Chloe asked, barely able to contain the love she felt for her family in that moment. She appealed to Lady Rathkenny's friends as she asked, "Will you take the word of your friend, who has no witnesses to the event, or that of an earl, a countess, a marquess, a marchioness, and a business owner?"

"No!" Lady Rathkenny burst into tears. "They're all lying. Everyone knows the O'Shea family is rotten to their core."

None of the others, including Lord and Lady Toome, looked convinced.

Lady Toome did make one last effort to get her way, though. "But if it wasn't the Duke of Blackburn in the outbuilding with Lady Rathkenny, who was it? And who was it who saw them?"

"I am the one who saw them," Lord Loughguile said,

raising his hand. "I'd had a bit too much to drink at supper and I stepped out for a bit of fresh air."

Chloe grimaced as she remembered exactly what that had meant.

"And I believe we have the solution to the identity of Lady Rathkenny's paramour," Christian said. "Michael, would you please join us?" he called over his shoulder. One of Kilrea Manor's young, handsome footmen stepped into the parlor with an expression of beautiful, exaggerated shame. He had the same dark hair as Deane and was of a similar height. "Michael, would you please tell us what you did on your night off the night before last."

"I met up with my sweetheart at her parents' house," Michael said, sending Lady Rathkenny a wink. "We had a right good time, didn't we, love?"

Lady Rathkenny let out a blood-curdling scream and sank to a pile of skirts and tears on the floor. "It's not true," she wailed. "It's not true at all. I made the whole thing up." She buried her face in her hands and wept.

"You...you made the *whole* thing up?" Lady Morrison asked.

"I did," Lady Rathkenny sobbed. "Blackburn never seduced me. Papa mentioned seeing someone, and I only said it was me in the outbuilding that night because I thought it would force him to marry me. I wanted to be a duchess." She dissolved into the most pathetic weeping Chloe had ever heard.

"So you haven't been diddling with this rather handsome footman?" Lady Loughguile asked.

"No, of course not," Lady Rathkenny snapped. She sucked in a breath and narrowed her damp, red-rimmed eyes at Chloe. "She must have been the one in the outbuilding. She's the harlot in this situation."

"Was Lady Chloe the woman you saw, Lord Loughguile?" Lady Toome asked hopefully.

"To be honest," Lord Loughguile drawled, "I was quite a bit in my cups that night. It could have been anyone."

That was the last piece of the picture that Chloe needed. She stepped up to Deane's side, taking his arm. "I suppose now is as good a time as any to make the announcement," she prompted him with a wink.

"I quite agree," Deane said. He turned to the others. "Lady Chloe and I are engaged to be married. This private family luncheon was to celebrate the happy occasion."

Lady Toome burst into tears along with Lady Rathkenny. "You horrible, wretched man. After everything I've done for you? I will never speak to you again. Never."

"If that is what you wish, aunt," Deane said. Chloe thought he looked rather relieved.

"You're welcome to stay here, at Kilrea Manor, for the rest of your time in Ireland," Christian offered. "My mother is away visiting her sister in Cork, so it wouldn't be much of an imposition."

"I would be happy to accept your offer, Lord Kilrea." Deane bowed regally to Christian.

"Michael, would you accompany Lord and Lady Toome home and bring back all of His Grace's things with you?" Christian went on.

"Certainly, my lord," Michael said with a perfect bow.

"I think we had all better return to our homes," Lord Toome said on behalf of everyone else. He was the only one who didn't look stunned or devastated or titillated by the entire scene. "Off you go now, one and all," he said, acting as shepherd and shooing all of the uninvited guests from the room.

Chloe and Deane and the rest of the combined forces of the O'Sheas parted like the Red Sea to allow Lord Toome and Lord Loughguile to escort the ladies out. Lady Toome and Lady Loughguile scooped the still-weeping Lady Rathkenny up under her arms and all but carried her out. The O'Shea contingent moved to the hall once they had all passed through the door, then waited until they were all well and truly gone before bursting into laughter.

"That Lady Rathkenny is quite a piece of work," Fergus said, shaking his head and turning his wheelchair toward the dining room. "You'd better count yourself lucky, Blackburn. If not for us, she might have led you to the altar by your nose."

"Don't I know it," Deane said, his eyes round with horror.

"Fortunately, the only one leading you to the altar by your nose will be me," Chloe said with a smile, hugging Deane's arm. "Although, as I have said before, with Cancer exerting such a strong influence in your horoscope, you will take to domestic bliss like a crab to water."

Chloe didn't even mind that several of her family members laughed.

"Welcome to this delightfully mad-capped family, Blackburn," Christian said as they made their way into the dining room, where luncheon was already laid out. "I was serious about my offer for you to stay here until you're ready to return to England. Even if that ends up being until this Christmas wedding I've heard so much about."

"I will gladly take you up on your offer, my lord," Deane replied with a nod and a smile.

Luncheon ended up being a joyful, noisy, and familial affair. Chloe loved how her sisters' husbands had dropped the trappings of politeness so quickly after marrying O'Sheas and become as loud and unruly as the rest of them, and she loved that Deane fit right in.

"Now that I'm marrying Chloe," he said to Shannon across the table, "I believe that leaves only you to find your way down the altar, Lady Shannon."

Shannon barked a laugh. "That is not something I plan to do anytime soon," she said.

"That's what you think," Fergus said in a low, wry voice, winking across the table to Henrietta.

Chloe wondered if they had some sort of plot in the

works or if they simply planned to exert all of their effort into finding Shannon a groom. Either way, it couldn't possibly have made Chloe any happier than she was. Everything had worked out perfectly in the end.

She said as much to Deane after lunch, as she went with him upstairs to the room one of Christian and Marie's maids had swiftly prepared for him.

"I couldn't have dreamed that my life would be this happy," she said with a dreamy sigh, stepping into the cozy guest room with Deane.

Evidently, Michael had managed to ride to Toome Hall and back, accomplishing his errand, while the family had been dining. Deane's traveling case rested on the bed, and his trunk lay at the foot of the bed.

"Neither could I," Deane said, ignoring his things to sweep Chloe into his arms. "It boggles my mind that I spent a good six weeks being dragged to one painful society event after another in search of some sort of brass ring when the real prize was right under my nose all along."

Chloe laughed, then sent him a teasing look and asked, "Are you referring to my diminutive size?"

"Not at all," Deane said. "I rather like your diminutive size." To prove it, he slipped his arms around her and held her close, tilting her chin up so that he could kiss her.

It was a glorious kiss. Chloe didn't think she would ever be able to get enough of Deane's kisses. They were magical, warm, and filled with starlight. The way he enveloped her and teased his tongue into her mouth to play with hers was both tender and possessive. She had never dreamed she would want to belong to a man until Deane came along.

He inched back with a spark in his eyes and said, "Do you think we are in any danger of being disturbed between now and supper?"

Chloe caught her breath, guessing exactly what he meant. "Colleen and Benedict have gone home, as have Fergus, Henrietta, and Shannon. I believe I heard Marie say she wanted to take a nap, and I'd wager Christian will take one with her. So no, I don't think we will be disturbed."

"Good," Deane said, letting go of her and rushing to the door to shut and lock it. "Because after the topsy-turvy day we've had so far, I'm feeling rather Scorpioesque."

Chloe laughed out loud, her body tingling with expectation as Deane dashed back across the room to remove his traveling case from the bed and throw back the coverings. "Scorpioesque is not a word," she said.

"Well, it should be," Deane said, undoing his tie and throwing it aside as he moved back to her. "As should be Geminiish and Cancerive."

Chloe laughed even more as she reached for the buttons of Deane's jacket to help the process along. "Perhaps, in addition to unlocking the mystery of the stars, we can rewrite the Dictionary next."

"That would be quite the endeavor," Deane laughed, pulling Chloe into his arms.

He took a moment to kiss her deeply and lingeringly before tugging the bottom of her blouse out of the band of her skirt. Chloe was glad she'd chosen not to dress up too elaborately for lunch with her family. It made it that much easier to undress with the least amount of fuss. Although what Deane had said their first time about undressing being the most utilitarian and least romantic part of lovemaking was absolutely true.

They managed to discard their clothes fast enough, though, and by the time they rolled into bed and between the cool, crisp sheets, Chloe was in heaven.

"We really shouldn't be doing this," she sighed, meaning exactly the opposite as Deane swept his hands up her arms, positioning them over her head, then kissed his way down her shoulder to her breasts. "At this rate, I'll take after Colleen and walk up the aisle already with child."

Deane popped his head up from where he'd been suckling and licking one of her nipples. "Lady Boleran was already with child at her wedding?"

Chloe nodded and giggled deep in her throat.

"Well, then," Deane said, grinding his body against hers in a way that left Chloe breathless and liquid, "we can't let the Bolerans outdo us. He's only a marquess, after all, and I'm a duke."

"Christmas is plenty of time for us to—oh!" Chloe

immediately lost track of what she'd been about to say as Deane returned to licking and sucking her nipple. She never would have guessed that her breasts were so closely connected to her sex, but the way he teased and fondled her with his mouth and hands had her core throbbing in no time.

"You are absolutely beautiful," Deane panted when he let her breast go, kissing his way down to her belly. "And I cannot wait to spend a lifetime doing extraordinarily wicked things to you."

"I cannot wait either," Chloe sighed as he shifted lower and pushed her thighs apart.

She was certain she must have looked ridiculous with her arms over her head and her legs parted wide, but the way Deane drank in the sight of her as he knelt between her legs said that he liked what he saw. He was impressive himself, all lean lines, broad shoulders and chest, trim waist, and powerful thighs. His prick stood up thick and tall with his balls drawn up underneath, which sent a delicious shiver through her. She'd never stopped to consider how arousing a man's body was until now, particularly since she knew exactly what he could do with it.

"You make it impossible for me to take my time," he said, covering her again and sliding his hand between their bodies to stroke her wet folds. Chloe gasped and purred as pleasure pulsed through her. "All I want to do is be inside of you, to be a part of you."

"Yes, please," she hummed, arching her hips into him. He didn't rush right into joining with her, but rather continued the work of his hand, stroking and circling her until she was panting and writhing, desperate for release.

"You are amazing," he murmured, his voice thick with lust, bending to kiss and nibble her neck as his hand continued its work. "You are the brightest star in the heavens to me."

Those beautiful words, combined with the work of his hands and mouth, sent her over the edge. Her body burst into a deep, throbbing orgasm that had her groaning with wonder and arching into him. It felt so good that she wished it would go on and on, and when he repositioned himself to surge into her, her pleasure renewed.

Deane moved in her with abandon, taking his pleasure from her as much as he gave. She loved how wild he was with her, how desperately he wanted her. She wrapped her arms and legs around him, urging him to let loose and take everything he wanted, she was more than willing to give it all. The sounds he made as he drew closer and closer to his own completion were the most magical thing Chloe had ever heard, and when his whole body tensed then released on a moan as he spilled himself into her, joy filled Chloe's heart.

"You are the most precious thing in the world to me," she panted, stroking his back and sides as he settled into exhaustion atop her, "and I love you dearly."

"I love you too," Deane hummed in satisfaction, "and we will be the happiest couple who ever lived."

EPILOGUE

*J*ust as all the rumors had predicted, a Christmas wedding for the Duke of Blackburn was announced before the end of the week. What no one in County Antrim had expected was for the bride to be one of those wicked O'Sheas. But memories were short, and grudges were easily dropped when an event like the wedding of a duke was set to take place.

"Everyone who was sent an invitation appears to be coming," Chloe said as she and Deane waited at the end of the dock in Belfast, where passengers disembarking the ferry from England stepped out to the street. "I would never have imagined that so many of the same ladies who have always turned up their noses at me would be interested in coming to my wedding."

Deane laughed. "That is because you are too good, my darling." He kissed her cheek, in spite of the subtle impropriety of the gesture in public. They'd done far more in private for the last six weeks and didn't plan to stop anytime soon. "You know most of them are coming in an attempt to ingratiate themselves to the new duchess."

"Who is the new—oh." Chloe laughed. She still hadn't adjusted to thinking of herself as a duchess. She didn't think she would ever feel like one. "I suppose I could be haughty and high-handed with them all, as they were with me," she said. "But I don't think that's in my nature."

"No, it isn't," Deane said, smiling down at her. "And that is just one of the many reasons I adore you."

"Oh, Deane," she smiled up at him, tucking herself against his side. She could blame it on the December cold, but truly, she just liked to be close to him. "You are a sweetheart."

"I am a devoted and loyal husband who is deeply in love with his wife," he said. "Or at least, I will be by this time next week."

He leaned in to kiss her in earnest, but before he could, a shout of, "Is that the sort of behavior befitting a duke?" rang out from the path leading from the dock to the street.

Deane jerked up and turned to a young man striding toward them as though he owned the world. Like Deane, he had dark hair and sparkling blue eyes, but he was younger and had a rascally look about him.

"Colin," Deane called out, stepping away from Chloe

so that he could meet his cousin and soon-to-be best man with a masculine embrace. "It's good to see you."

"It's good to be seen," Colin replied, thumping Deane's back, then turning to Chloe. "And I take it this is your beautiful bride?"

Chloe liked Lord Colin Crenshaw immediately. Deane had been telling her about him for weeks—about how their fathers were brothers, how Colin was ten years younger than him but like a brother all the same, and how much trouble Colin had managed to get into in his twenty-two years of life. But it was the young man's smile and effusive good humor that Chloe liked at once.

"I've heard so much about you," Chloe greeted him like she would her brother, kissing his cheek. "Deane warned me that you are a Sagittarius, but I'm certain we will get along as best of friends all the same."

"I certainly hope so," Colin said, kissing her cheek back as though they'd been friends for years. "I say, Deane, you certainly know how to find them. This bride of yours is the most delicious thing I've seen all year. Does she have a sister?"

Chloe was certain he was joking, and Deane laughed, but it was also at exactly that moment that Shannon came marching around a corner, looking as though she were ready to start a brawl in the street. Chloe had forgotten entirely that Shannon was due to make a trip into Belfast that day as well for her brewing business, otherwise she would have offered her sister a ride. Although on second thought, driving such a long way with Shannon when she was in a temper never made for a comfortable ride. As soon as Shannon spotted them, she started in surprise, then crossed the street to join them.

"That oaf at McGinty's Pub had some nerve, turning me away when he's been doing business with me by correspondence for months now," Shannon growled without a greeting. "I have half a mind to spit in the next shipment of beer I sent to him, or worse."

Colin's eyes widened, and he swept Shannon with a look from head to toe and said, "Why, hello, and aren't you lovely," with a look in his eyes as though he wanted to take a bite out of her.

Chloe raised a hand to her mouth to hide her laughter.

Shannon's scowl deepened as she stared back at Colin. Her back was already up, but the bold and flirtatious way Deane's young cousin greeted her only aggravated her more. "And just who in blazes do you think you are?"

"Your future husband," Colin answered, dropping to one knee. "If you'll have me." The look Colin sent her was both silly and sensual.

Shannon turned a flat look to Deane. "Who is this ridiculous boy?" she asked.

Deane cleared his throat. "Colin, get up," he said out of the corner of his mouth. When Colin bounded to his feet, Deane went on with, "Lady Shannon, this is my cousin, Lord Colin Crenshaw, Earl of Stamford."

"This pup is an earl?" Shannon asked, blinking at Colin.

"I am," Colin said, "though I'll be a marquess some-day, when my dear father passes, if you can wait for that." He batted his eyelashes at Shannon as prettily as any painted coquette, nearly causing Chloe to snort with laughter.

Deane cleared his throat and went on with, "Colin, this is Lady Shannon O'Shea, Chloe's eldest sister."

Colin gasped dramatically. "She *does* have a sister," he said, stars in his eyes. "I can already tell this will be the most auspicious holiday of my life."

Shannon sighed and rolled her eyes, though Chloe thought she detected a hint of amusement from her. "And this is turning out to be the worst day of my life," she said, stepping away from them. "My wagon is parked just over there, so you will excuse me if I do not stay to indulge in chit-chat. I'm ready to go home."

"And I'm ready to go with you," Colin said, following her.

Chloe finally let herself burst into laughter. "I think we're going to have our hands full for this wedding," she told Deane.

Deane sighed and shook his head, but Chloe could see the joy in his eyes. "I think we will too. Colin is a handful in the best of times, and he's already quite taken with your sister."

"Oy! You!" One of the dockworkers called after Colin. "What about all this baggage?"

Colin was still flirting away with Shannon on the other side of the street, but turned to wave at the dockworker.

"We'd better see to things for him," Deane said with a laugh. He turned and offered his arm so they could walk over to the pile of baggage coming off the ferry.

"He won't toy with Shannon and be false with her, will he?" Chloe asked with concern.

"Colin?" Deane shrugged, then shook his head. "He's actually an incredibly morally sound young man. He just likes to have fun. And even though he is a favorite with the ladies, I've never seen him propose to one at first sight, like he just did with your sister."

"As long as he won't hurt her," Chloe said, smiling at her sister's back as she tried to shoo Colin away, "I, for one, am very interested to see how this comedy unfolds."

———

I HOPE YOU'VE ENJOYED CHLOE AND DEANE'S STORY! But what about Shannon and the irascible Lord Colin Crenshaw? Can a determined businesswoman like Shannon warm up to the antics of the younger man, Colin? Or will his high spirits during the course of the wedding drive her out of her mind...and right into his arms? Find out in *Earls Just Wanna Have Fun*! Keep clicking to get started on Chapter One!

. . .

IF YOU ENJOYED THIS BOOK AND WOULD LIKE TO HEAR more from me, please sign up for my newsletter! When you sign up, you'll get a free, full-length novella, *A Passionate Deception*. Victorian identity theft has never been so exciting in this story of hope, tricks, and starting over. Part of my West Meets East series, *A Passionate Deception* can be read as a stand-alone. Pick up your free copy today by signing up to receive my newsletter (which I only send out when I have a new release)!

Sign up here: http://eepurl.com/cbaVMH

ARE YOU ON SOCIAL MEDIA? I AM! COME AND JOIN the fun on Facebook: http://www. facebook.com/merryfarmerreaders

I'M ALSO A HUGE FAN OF INSTAGRAM AND POST LOTS of original content there: https://www. instagram.com/merryfarmer/

AND NOW, GET STARTED FOR EARLS JUST WANNA HAVE FUN....

BELFAST, IRELAND – DECEMBER 1888

.   .   .

LADY SHANNON O'SHEA MIGHT HAVE BEEN THE eldest sister of a prominent earl, she might have had one sister married to an earl, one married to a marquess, and a third engaged to a duke, but she was not going to let that stop her from being a woman in her own right, and a businesswoman at that. And she most certainly wasn't about to let her brother, Lord Fergus O'Shea, trap her into a marriage the way he had with their sisters. If anyone was to steer the course of Shannon's life, it would be herself.

Although that effort was not proceeding with the speed and ease that she would have liked it to as she stood toe to toe with one William McGinty in the backroom of McGinty's Pub in Belfast.

"We have been doing business by correspondence for months now, Mr. McGinty. Nearly a year," Shannon argued, fists planted on her hips, fire in her eyes.

"I have been doing business with a Mr. Shannon O'Shea for these past several months," Mr. McGinty said, arms crossed, a wry, irritating grin on his face that hinted he thought the entire argument were a joke. "Where is that Mr. O'Shea?"

"He is here, sir." Shannon stood straighter, glaring at the man with what she hoped was the full authority of her class. Not that class had done her a lick of good in her thirty years of life. "You have been doing business with me. Lady Shannon O'Shea."

"Lady Shannon O'Shea?" Mr. McGinty's eyes went wide and his smile grew. "You're a bloody nob on top of everything else?"

Shannon huffed out an impatient breath and pressed her fingertips to the headache forming behind her temples. "I am a businesswoman," she insisted. "I own O'Shea's Brewery, an endeavor that I started with my sisters several years ago."

"Your sisters?" Mr. McGinty laughed outright, clutching his belly.

"Do not mock or deride me, sir," Shannon snapped. "Yes, it is true that brewing began as a simply hobby to keep the four of us occupied, but we became quite good at it. My sisters might have moved on to other hobbies—" if marriage and childrearing could even be considered hobbies, "—but I continued on with it. I studied every text I could get my hands on. I have corresponded with some of the largest breweries in Ireland, England, and America to perfect my art. I have experimented and made use of hops and barley from every corner of Europe. And you have been gladly purchasing and serving my beer for these many months now."

"True, but I had no idea it was made by women," Mr. McGinty laughed. "And ladies at that."

Shannon loathed the man for the way he snorted and guffawed. He wasn't even looking down his nose at her, as if a lady wasn't worthy of his derision.

"I will have you know," she said in a tight, clipped voice, "that women have been brewers for centuries. In the Middle Ages, the profession of brewing beer was exclusively a female endeavor. Men had nothing to do with it. They guarded their secrets and passed their art down through guilds that were tightly regulated. And now you would go against centuries of established tradition by refusing to do business with me?"

Mr. McGinty finished laughing and pulled out a handkerchief to wipe his eyes. He made a sound of enjoyment, still treating Shannon and the thing she held dearest to her heart as something funny he'd read in the papers. "Look," he said, sniffed, put his handkerchief away, and went back to crossing his arms. "I'll continue to sell your beer in my pub, if that's what you want."

"What I want is a distribution deal so that you sell my beer in all of the pubs you own throughout the northern part of Ireland," Shannon said.

"And you think you can keep up with that sort of demand?" Mr. McGinty's brow flew up.

"Yes," Shannon insisted, "because what I also want, what we have been discussing through correspondence these many months now, is to merge your brewery with mine so that both businesses can be expanded to serve a wider area."

"No," Mr. McGinty said without so much as letting her explain her reasons. "I'm not going into business with a noblewoman."

"But you have not even read my proposal." Shannon reached into the satchel she had slung over one shoulder, intending to pull out the sheaf of papers on which her proposal and projections for profit and production were written.

"No," Mr. McGinty stopped her in a slightly more

forceful voice. "I'm not interested in any of it."

"But you were interested," she argued. "Your letters said you were exceptionally interested."

"Interested going into business with a Mr. Shannon O'Shea," Mr. McGinty matched her peevish tone.

"I am Shannon O'Shea," Shannon growled.

"Not the one I thought I was talking to," Mr. McGinty snapped with an air of finality. "Now, go away, your ladyship."

"You have not seen my proposal yet." Shannon was determined to be heard. She took the proposal pages from her satchel and shook them at Mr. McGinty. "Once you read this, I'm certain you will see—"

"I am not interested, my lady," Mr. McGinty roared, leaning closer to her. "Get out of my pub before I call the police to have you removed forcibly."

"But you haven't—"

"Go and find yourself some titled toff to marry." Mr. McGinty pointed to the back door. "Go out and buy a bunch of lovely, pretty dresses and have yourself a tea party with your friends."

"I do not have any friends," Shannon growled, glaring at the man.

He turned her words on her by leaning toward her, meeting her eyes, and saying, "Maybe that is your problem. Go!" He pointed to the door again.

Shannon squeezed the papers in her hand so hard she crumpled them. It simply wasn't fair. After all of the efforts and overtures she'd made, after all of the letters she'd written and all of the recipes she'd perfected, she was unable to do more with her business than call it a quaint little hobby, and all because she was a woman.

She glared at Mr. McGinty one more time before turning and marching out of his pub and into the alley behind it without so much as giving the man the dignity of taking her leave. Once she made it out of the alley and into the street where McGinty's pub, and several others, stood, her anger burst and she deflated into sullenness.

All over Europe and America, women were making incredible strides. They were able to attend university in many places. Women were graduating medical school and becoming doctors. Middle class women were taking jobs as secretaries and postmistresses and the like at a rate that alarmed men. There were even several enterprising women in England and America who had made fortunes for themselves as businesswomen, selling things such as cosmetics, grooming products, and household goods. Times were changing, and the future for women seemed bright.

But some dolt in a third-rate pub in Belfast wouldn't even speak to her about expanding her business so that she could join the ranks of new female entrepreneurs. It was enough to make Shannon want to shout in frustration and kick the wall of the nearest building—something she didn't do, because at least she had her dignity. So much was changing, and yet it was painfully the same as always that men insisted on only doing business with other men.

She fostered the anger boiling in her gut as she walked back to the seaside street where she'd been forced to park her wagon earlier. She'd brought sample kegs of her beer with her, and had given most of them to Mr. McGinty. More beer was brewing at home, in the cottage Shannon had shared with her sisters during the years Fergus had been in England, but a cottage industry like that would never be enough to support her business dreams.

She let out a sigh as she turned a corner and headed along the street that faced one of the docks where ferries coming from England put in. A ferry was there now, its passenger disembarking. In her heart, Shannon knew that a good half of her anger was not directed toward Mr. McGinty and his like at all, but rather was directed at her sisters. They'd had such a lively, cozy, fun life when the four of them were living at the cottage together. It had been the perfect arrangement for independent-minded women, like the four of them. As the oldest, Shannon had felt like the mother hen, taking care of Chloe, Colleen, and Marie as if they were her own.

Now they were all gone, or nearly gone. They betrayed their solemn oath that the four of them would never marry and that they would spend their lives together, independently. Marie had her earl and was expecting her first child at Kilrea Manor. Colleen was also with child, a marchioness with a grand estate to oversee. And stary-eyed baby of the family, Chloe, was about to marry an English duke in one week. The Christmas wedding was the talk of the county, but Shannon could only think about afterward, when Chloe and her duke would move back to England to fulfill his duties.

They'd all left her, all three of them. And how long would it be until Fergus went back to England to tend to the duties that his English wife still had in managing her late husband's estates for the benefit of their son? In the blink of an eye, they would all be gone, and what would Shannon be left with?

As she drew near her wagon, a commotion from the other side of the street, near the exit of the ferry dock, caught her attention. Her heart lurched in her chest as she spotted Chloe and her groom, the Duke of Blackburn. Another man had just joined them from the ferry. Shannon was reminded that Blackburn's cousin was due to arrive that day from England, to take up duties as the duke's best man for the wedding. Well, Shannon wasn't about to let the man charge in, full of English stuffiness and superiority, and ruin her sister's wedding, her Christmas, and, if things continued on the way they had been lately, her life.

She crossed the street, shoulders squared, and approached the trio.

WANT TO READ MORE?
PICK UP EARLS JUST WANNA HAVE FUN
TODAY!

ABOUT THE AUTHOR

I hope you have enjoyed *If You Wannabe My Marquess*. If you'd like to be the first to learn about when new books in the series come out and more, please sign up for my newsletter here: http://eepurl.com/cbaVMH And remember, Read it, Review it, Share it! For a complete list of works by Merry Farmer with links, please visit http://wp.me/P5ttjb-14F.

Merry Farmer is an award-winning novelist who lives in suburban Philadelphia with her cats, Justine and Peter. She has been writing since she was ten years old and realized one day that she didn't have to wait for the teacher to assign a creative writing project to write something. It was the best day of her life. She then went on to earn not one but two degrees in History so that she would always have something to write about. Her books have reached the Top 100 at Amazon, iBooks, and Barnes & Noble, and have been named finalists in the prestigious RONE and Rom Com Reader's Crown awards.

ACKNOWLEDGMENTS

I owe a huge debt of gratitude to my awesome beta-readers, Caroline Lee and Jolene Stewart, for their suggestions and advice. And double thanks to Julie Tague, for being a truly excellent editor and to Cindy Jackson for being an awesome assistant!

Click here for a complete list of other works by Merry Farmer.

Printed in Great Britain
by Amazon